When the final farewell scene arrived. . .

Phillip swept her into his arms, captured her lips with his own, and kissed her soundly. It took her breath away, and she hadn't fully recovered by the time the curtain began its ascent for their bows. A roar of applause thundered through the auditorium as the actors joined hands, stepped forward, and all of them bent in unison for a final ovation.

"What were you thinking?" she asked as they continued bowing. . . .

"I was thinking about making the play as realistic as possible. It would have been obvious to the audience if I had only pretended to kiss you," he said, while giving her a broad smile. . . .

She remained silent, knowing she dare not speak the truth. He would surely be appalled to hear that his kiss had sent ripples of excitement coursing through her body, that she had enjoyed the excitement of his lips against her own, and that she was still taking pleasure in the warmth of his kiss that lingered on her lips. Or would he be so horrified? The kiss had seemed genuine; yet, when questioned, he had been swift to say that he was merely acting his part. Why was she even entertaining such silly thoughts? A man was interested in having only a pretty woman on his arm, one that caused heads to turn, and she, with her plain face and imperfect figure, could never be such a woman.

JUDITH McCOY MILLER was chosen favorite new author in the Heartsong series, and her historical novels have ranked high among readers. She makes her home in Kansas with her family and is a certified legal assistant.

Books by Judith McCoy Miller

Sleigh
Bells

Judith McCoy Miller

Heartsong Presents

To Sondra Boyer—friend, confidante, and genuine seeker. Isn't He wonderful!

Special Thanks to Raymond Dunn for his time, energy, and assistance in curing my computers of their many ills; and to Gaylynn Childs, Geary County historian, for her valuable assistance, knowledge, and information regarding Junction City, Fort Riley, and Geary County.

A note from the author:
I love to hear from my readers! You may correspond with me by writing: **Judith McCoy Miller**
Author Relations
PO Box 719
Uhrichsville, OH 44683

ISBN 1-58660-071-0

SLEIGH BELLS

All Scripture quotations are taken from the King James Version of the Bible.

Cover illustration by Gary Maria.

PRINTED IN THE U.S.A.

one

Fort Riley, Kansas—October 1870

Theodora Yorke stared out across the parade field, where her father was leading his unit through the rigors of cavalry tactical training. The soldiers, in their blue, wool uniforms and buffalo coats, appeared unaffected by the light snow that had been falling for several hours and now dusted the ground. Plumes of cold air fanned out from the horses' nostrils, and steam rose off the animals' glistening bodies as they snorted and raced back and forth across the field, the soldiers drawing their sabers in mock battle.

"How much longer is Father going to keep those poor men out there? At this rate, they'll all be admitted to the hospital by nightfall," Teddi complained.

"You seem a bit agitated, my dear. Your father isn't drilling the men any longer than normal, and they're not going to freeze. It's more likely they are overly warm in those heavy buffalo coats. Do move away from the window and come have some tea," her mother replied as the maid carried a flowered porcelain teapot and cups into the parlor and, with a practiced ease, placed each piece of the tea service on the cloth-covered table. "Sitting there with your nose pressed to that frosty windowpane isn't going to hurry him along."

Teddi rose from the chair and absently moved about the room. She straightened the tatted edge of a doily, then moved a vase from the small, marble-top table beside the sofa to one end of the thick wood mantle before returning it to its original position. Moving back toward the mantle, she ran her finger

along the metal stripping on the edge of the fire screen standing in front of the fireplace. Startled by the heat, she hastily
stuck the finger in her mouth.

"A bit warmer than you anticipated?" her mother asked
with a chuckle.

"What? Oh, my finger. . . Yes, I didn't think about the
metal being so hot," Teddi replied as she walked back toward
the window.

"Teddi, *please* come over here and sit down," Isabelle urged.
"Let's have our tea; perhaps your father will complete his
training exercises, and the two of you can be off to the train
station by the time we've finished."

Isabelle Yorke smiled at her youngest child. After giving
birth to four sons, Isabelle had given up on the idea of ever
having a daughter. During her final pregnancy, Isabelle had
been determined she would not be disappointed with another
son. In fact, she had done everything in her power to avoid
thinking the possibility even existed that she might give birth
to a daughter. In keeping with that decision, she chose a suitable name for the yet unborn child—Theodore Edward.
When the midwife announced that she'd had a daughter,
Isabelle held fast to the name she had chosen for the baby.
Clayton had briefly suggested that they name their daughter
Lydia, after an old family friend, but Isabelle said they would
merely alter the name to Theodora Edwina. It hadn't taken
long for the baby girl's four older brothers to nickname their
little sister Teddi. And that moniker had remained.

Jonathan, their youngest son, had just turned four, and
William, the eldest, had been twelve when Isabelle gave
birth to the long-awaited baby girl. Smiling as she recalled
those fond memories, Isabelle once again beckoned her
daughter to the tea table. That darling baby girl had grown
into the independent-thinking, twenty-two-year-old woman
who now walked toward her.

Because Teddi was the only girl among four boys, Isabelle and Clayton had understandably taken great pleasure in indulging their daughter. Fortunately for all of them, Teddi was not a demanding child, and, through no effort of her parents', their little girl had not become the spoiled, petulant child that one would have expected. She was bright and well mannered, although she was more of a tomboy than Isabelle would have preferred. But, as Clayton was always quick to point out, what could one expect with four older brothers and a father who enjoyed boisterous play? Isabelle was pleased that Teddi had acquired her stylish taste in clothing and home decor, but it was evident to even the casual observer that Teddi Yorke's physical appearance was not inherited from her stunning mother.

Teddi stood at the window and pulled back the heavy, burgundy drape for one final glance. With a long, deep sigh, she allowed the curtain to fall back into place as she walked to the table, sat down, and began stirring her cup of tea with a vengeance.

"You certainly are out of sorts today. Is your grumpy behavior due to the fact that your father wouldn't share his secret?" Isabelle inquired as she poured a splash of cream into her steaming cup of tea.

"I don't think he has a secret. I think he just wants company when he goes to the train station. Now that I've agreed to go, he's bound and determined to keep me waiting. At this rate, I won't get anything accomplished this morning. I really should be at the hospital checking on patients. You *know* those two orderlies won't take care of things properly."

"I'm sure the hospital will be just fine without you for one morning. Besides, those few patients should be ready to return to duty soon, shouldn't they?"

"Well, yes," Teddi admitted begrudgingly. "But they are still entitled to decent care until their release. After all, they've had only the most rudimentary medical treatment as it is."

"I wouldn't say that! You're an *excellent* nurse, and the hospital is very fortunate to have you—especially during these past few months."

"Having me available is not the same as having a qualified doctor on hand," Teddi argued.

"Perhaps. But I'd wager those young men would much rather have you caring for them than all the doctors the military has to offer."

Teddi smiled. "Only because I spend more time listening to their complaints. But thank you, Mother. You always seem to cheer me. I'm sorry I've been acting like such a bore."

"Here's your father now," Isabelle said as she rose from the table and greeted her husband with a warm embrace. "Ohhh, your face feels like a chunk of ice!" she exclaimed, pulling away and shaking her finger at him when he persisted and buried his freezing face in her neck.

Teddi laughed at her parents' antics but fled when Clayton headed in her direction. "Afraid of a little cold?" her father called after her when she took refuge in the dining room. "Better get your warmest cloak, and then let's get going. The train should be arriving soon."

Teddi shook her head as she walked into the parlor. "I've been waiting for an hour; he's home for one minute and tells me *I* should hurry," Teddi said to her mother, feigning indignation.

"Oh, you know how he is. Just because he's a general, he thinks everyone should jump to his command," Isabelle replied, giving her husband a mock salute.

"What is this? The two of you carrying on a conversation about me as though I'm not even in the room?" Clayton asked, unable to keep the sparkle out of his eyes. "You continue with *that* behavior and you'll never know my secret," he teased.

"I don't think you *have* a secret. I think you just want company going to the train station," Teddi countered as she fastened her fur-trimmed, red, wool cloak. Pulling the matching fur-trimmed hat down on her head, she peeked up at her father. "I'm right, aren't I?"

"No, you're *not* right. But if you'd rather stay home. . ."

"I didn't say I wanted to stay home. I'm coming. See?" Teddi asked, holding out her hands to emphasize the fact that she was pulling on her gloves. "We'll be back soon, Mother. Are we bringing the surprise home for Mother to see?"

"Yes, as a matter-of-fact, I believe we'll do just that," Clayton replied while he winked at Isabelle.

"I saw that! Do you know what the surprise is, Mother? You do, don't you? And you've let me stew and fret all morning, acting like you didn't know a thing!"

"Go along with your father, Teddi; don't concern yourselves if the train is late. I'll have Florence hold the noonday meal until your return," Isabelle replied, ignoring her daughter's question and walking off toward the kitchen at the rear of the house.

‹∂

A gust of wind whipped across the open expanse of the parade grounds, and Teddi snuggled more deeply under the heavy, wool lap robe. Her father gave her a grin as he flicked the reins and the team of horses pulled the sleigh into motion. "First sleigh ride of the winter. Are you warm enough?" he cheerily inquired.

Teddi nodded. "You *do* love winter, don't your, Father?" she asked, giving him a broad smile.

"Best season of the year, as far as I'm concerned. I've always loved the snow and cold weather—and then there's Christmas, of course," he replied with a wink.

She shivered as the unrelenting wind whipped the blanket and a gush of cold air rushed down her neck. "Christmas is two months away. I think we could agree that winter has arrived, even if the snow holds off a little while longer."

"Perhaps. But the more snow, the better, as far as I'm concerned," he replied, puffs of frosty air billowing forth with each word he spoke. "Pull my buffalo robe over you if you're cold," he offered, pointing toward the furry animal hide lying on the opposite seat. "We'll be in Junction City soon."

It was too cold to carry on a conversation, Teddi decided. Besides, the only thing she really wanted to know, her father wouldn't tell her. He'd been teasing and dropping hints about his surprise for the last three weeks, much as he did as Christmas approached each year. Her father loved keeping secrets even more than he loved wintertime! And this secret was particularly annoying because she hadn't been able to figure out even one of the clues her father had given.

At first she had thought her brother Jonathan was coming home for a visit before he began his military assignment at Washington Barracks in Washington City, D.C. When her father had told her that she was wrong, Teddi had been extremely disappointed. General Yorke was devout in his Christian convictions, and his daughter knew he wouldn't lie. It had always been a strict rule in the Yorke household that lying would not be tolerated. The children grew up memorizing Bible verses, but Clayton and Isabelle were in agreement that it was most important that the children also put those memory verses into practice. Never ones to believe that their children should look elsewhere for a good example, the Yorkes practiced what they preached.

Even on the few occasions when one of the children would correctly guess a Christmas surprise, Clayton would readily admit to the truth. This, of course, caused no end of difficulty for Isabelle. Knowing the disappointment her children would experience if they had no surprise on Christmas morning, Isabelle would scurry about, attempting to find some other exciting yet inexpensive Christmas gift. On each such occasion, Isabelle had been successful, serving to reinforce Clayton's stance that no matter what the circumstances, telling the truth was the best policy.

Hearing that Jonathan would not be on the train seemed to suddenly deepen Teddi's longing to see him. She had formed a close relationship with her youngest brother as they were growing up. Her other brothers had been gone from home by the time she was old enough to become a pesky little sister. She was sure there was no one quite as wonderful as Jonathan, and when he left for college, she was sure she would die of loneliness. Then, after three years of school, he came home and announced he was planning to attend the United States Military Academy at West Point. Although Clayton had been sure that the boy would change his mind when they received word he would be required to enter the academy as a freshman, Jonathan had been undeterred, and Teddi had been distraught that he would once again be leaving.

Since his departure to the academy over four years ago, he had come home for only one visit. Teddi had fervently hoped he would return after graduation last spring, but once again she had been disappointed. They had received a letter shortly before his graduation, advising that he had received orders to report to Washington City, D.C., and there would be no time for him to return home for a visit. Her parents had taken it in stride, saying it was a part of military life, but not Teddi. *Likely, we'll never see each other again*, Teddi thought, knowing her father would chuckle and call her melodramatic if she voiced her opinion. Smiling, she waved at a couple of young boys with ice skates slung over their shoulders as they headed toward the river.

"That ice isn't thick enough for skating," her father called out to the boys as their sleigh continued onward across the Republican River Bridge.

Perhaps she could visit Jonathan in Washington next spring after he had an opportunity to settle into his new command. After all, Aunt Nina and Uncle Frederick lived in the nation's capital, and she could stay with them during her visit. She would discuss the idea with her mother when they returned home. Just thinking of the prospective visit warmed Teddi's spirits.

"Here we are," her father announced as he pulled back on the reins, drawing the team to a halt. The horses perked their ears at the sound of a train's shrill whistle in the distance. "Won't be long now." He gave Teddi a broad grin as he tied the reins to a rough wooden hitching rail and then returned to assist her out of the sleigh. "Let's go into the station and wait. I'm sure Harold has a fire burning that will warm you."

Teddi didn't hesitate. Stepping down, she quickly grabbed her father's arm and rushed toward the depot. An iron, pot-bellied stove stuffed with wood sat in the center of the room, the firebox glowing a bright reddish orange.

"Better get the lid off that pail," Clayton hollered in greeting to the stationmaster. Teddi looked toward the stove and spotted a syrup bucket sitting on top of the heating device.

"Thanks, Clayton. I meant to take the lid off that bucket, but then I got busy," Harold replied, stepping quickly toward the bucket and carefully removing the lid. He peered into the container and then gave them a smile. "Good thing you came in. My soup's already boiling. A minute or two more and we'd have had us one fine explosion! I'd be cleaning up soup for days to come."

Teddi took a deep whiff of what smelled like a savory beef and barley concoction. The pleasurable aroma and her growling stomach served as a reminder that it was past noon, and, except for a few bites of leftover cornbread that she'd grabbed while passing through the kitchen much earlier in the day, she'd not yet eaten.

"What brings you into town in this cold weather?" Harold asked while Teddi moved closer to the heating stove and held her hands out toward its warmth.

"Meeting the train," Clayton replied. "Can't tell you any more than that, or I'd spoil Teddi's surprise."

Harold nodded and motioned Clayton to come nearer. Teddi watched as the two men leaned closely together and spoke in hushed tones. A few moments later, Harold slapped Clayton on the back, and the two men shared a deep belly laugh. Teddi shook her head at the men and turned away. She was determined not to ask any more questions about her father's surprise.

"Won't have to wait much longer," Harold chortled as the train slowly chugged closer to the depot. "I'd better get out there," he said, pulling his heavy coat from a peg and then shoving his arms into the sleeves of the woolen jacket.

A gush of cold air and featherlight snow surged into the room, causing Teddi once again to retreat toward the black iron stove. "Don't you want to go out to the platform and wait? The train's coming to a stop," her father urged, obviously anxious for her to catch an immediate glimpse of the secret.

"Too cold out there—you go ahead," she smugly replied. She wasn't about to let her father have any more satisfaction than he'd already enjoyed with his mysterious surprise!

two

Captain Phillip Hamilton leaned forward and peered out the dirty train window that was now frosted from the cold. He felt as though he'd been traveling for months, although his journey had taken only a week and had even permitted him the luxury of a relaxing overnight stay in St. Louis. Now his dark blue uniform was rumpled, and his calf-high, black boots had lost their luster. Nothing a good spit-shine wouldn't fix, but there would be no time for such last-minute repairs before his arrival in Junction City.

He leaned back against the hard, wooden seat, ran his fingers through his thick, chocolate-brown hair, and once again told himself that he'd made a sound decision. Fort Riley would be a new beginning, his first assignment as a military chaplain. A new beginning with a few old friends to assist him with his adjustment to army life on the prairie.

How long had it been? At least seven or eight years since he and Jonathan Yorke had become best friends at Fort McHenry, where their fathers had both been serving as army officers. They had attended high school together, and when Phillip's parents were required to leave for their new military assignment two weeks before graduation, Phillip had remained behind with the Yorkes. They had been his surrogate parents that summer before both boys left for college.

The boys had formed a rare friendship that had not dimmed through the years. They had remained in contact and enjoyed occasional visits, although their fathers had never again been stationed at the same military post. In fact, Phillip had managed a visit to West Point for Jonathan's graduation ceremonies in the spring. Each of them was still amazed that the other had chosen a military career. Unhappy with the separations that the military had caused in their lives, both boys had vowed never to choose such a career. Now, however, they were both officers in the United States Army. Phillip smiled at the thought.

The train slowed and then lurched to a stop a short time later. *Well, here goes,* he thought, *the start of my life in the vast, open spaces of the West*. Picking his way down the narrow aisle of the train, he slung a canvas bag over his shoulder and grabbed his black leather satchel before disembarking.

"Phillip!" a resonant bass voice called out. "Over here."

Phillip turned and caught sight of General Yorke. It didn't appear that the general had changed a bit. Perhaps the laugh lines around his mouth and eyes had grown a little deeper, and a few gray strands were woven into his dark hair, but Phillip would have recognized Clayton Yorke anywhere.

"Good to see you, sir," Phillip said, raising his arm in a smart salute.

"Plenty of time for the formalities of military protocol later. Come here, boy," he said, pulling Phillip into a bear hug. "It's good to see you. I can't tell you how pleased I was when I heard that you had requested to serve at Fort Riley."

"Thank you, sir. I'm sure it will be one of my most pleasurable assignments. Although I must admit I hadn't expected the cold temperature—not at the end of October."

"This is Kansas, my boy. The weather changes here more often than most of us change our underwear," Clayton replied, giving a hearty laugh. "Don't tell the missus I said that. She'd have my hide," he continued, emitting another deep belly laugh. "Come on inside. Got someone in there you're probably going to enjoy seeing again."

Teddi's head snapped upward as the depot door swung open, permitting entry to a cold gust of wind, along with her father and another army officer. She glanced toward her father's hands. He wasn't carrying anything. Perhaps his surprise hadn't arrived after all.

"Look familiar?" General Yorke inquired, nodding toward his daughter, then looking back at Phillip.

Phillip looked more closely at the young woman, attempting to discern who she was, and hopeful he could give General Yorke the answer he was seeking. She wasn't overly attractive. In fact, her nose was rather large, and she was somewhat thick-waisted. He forced himself to concentrate. She reminded him of someone. Just then, she turned and looked him square in the eyes. Jonathan! She looked like Jonathan.

"Teddi?" he questioned the general.

"Yes indeed, our little Teddi—all grown up. Come here and take a good look at this fellow," Clayton urged his daughter.

Teddi rose from the bench near the warm stove and hesitantly moved toward the two men as she narrowed her eyes and surveyed the visitor. She was only inches away when she looked deep into the velvet-brown eyes and then quickly turned toward her father. "Phillip?" she inquired.

"None other," her father proudly replied. "Now how's that for a surprise?"

Phillip gave her a weak smile. *He* was the surprise for Teddi Yorke? Somehow he didn't quite understand what kind of surprise he could possibly be, and he wasn't sure he wanted an explanation—at least not until he was alone with the general.

Not sure what else to do, Phillip proffered his hand. "Good to see you again, Teddi. You were just a young girl the last time I saw you. In fact, you probably hardly remember me at all," he said, continuing to pump her arm up and down until she finally pulled her hand from his.

"I remember you, Phillip," she replied, giving him a feeble smile and then turned to look at her father in what appeared to be utter confusion.

"Really? You would have only been twelve or thirteen years old when I last saw you," he said, grappling to make polite conversation.

"Is this another matchmaking attempt that you merely decided to call a surprise?" Teddi whispered to her father.

Clayton gave her a warning look. "In addition to Phillip's arrival being a surprise, he has news that will certainly be of interest to you. Tell her, Phillip," the general commanded, ignoring his daughter's question.

"Tell her what?" Phillip inquired, clearly confused by the conversation.

"Oh, never mind. I'll tell her. Phillip is our new doctor and chaplain. He's been assigned to Fort Riley. There. . .now isn't that a fine surprise?"

"*You're* going to be the post surgeon?" Teddi asked.

Phillip thought she sounded as though that were an incredible idea. He glanced back and forth between father and daughter. Something had gone amiss, but he wasn't quite sure just why his being a doctor would cause Teddi such surprise.

"Physician *and* chaplain. At least that's what my orders state. Beginning Monday morning," Phillip answered.

"And none too soon, I might add. We've been without a doctor for nearly three months. Isn't that correct, my dear?" Clayton inquired.

"Four months. But we already have an excellent chaplain. Are we ready to go home now? I'm sure Mother is anxious for our return," Teddi urged.

"Have I done something to offend you?" Phillip asked once they had climbed into the sleigh and were headed back toward the post. He wasn't an expert in matters concerning women, but he certainly realized that the chill in the air was caused by more than the unseemly Kansas weather.

"Since your arrival a few moments ago? Of course not.

I'm merely anxious to get home and have lunch," Teddi answered.

He gazed at her, certain that something was amiss. But surely she would have told him so. There would be no reason to keep him in the dark. Besides, what could he possibly have done to vex anyone? He'd been off the train for only a few minutes. There must be some plausible answer. Maybe Jonathan had spoken ill of him to Teddi, or perhaps it was some childhood prank he and Jonathan had played years ago that she hadn't forgotten. But that didn't make any sense. She would have been a gangly, twelve or thirteen year old and surely would have forgotten a childhood prank by now. His forehead creased into a frown as he continued to stare at her profile; all the while, she ignored him, gazing at the passing countryside.

"You look as though you're deep in thought, Phillip," Clayton called over his shoulder as he urged the horses toward home. "You two should be busy talking—getting caught up on old times."

Teddi turned, gave Phillip a perfunctory half-smile, and then glared at her father. "Phillip is Jonathan's friend. They would be the ones needing to catch up on old times, not the two of us," Teddi explained, sounding like an exasperated schoolteacher attempting to teach the class dunce a rudimentary lesson.

Clayton ignored his daughter's arresting glance and continued as though she'd not spoken. "If you don't want to talk about old times, Teddi, the least you could do is tell Phillip about the hospital and his waiting patients."

"I'm sure Phillip would rather make his own assessments once he's arrived at the hospital."

"You mentioned there is already a chaplain at the post?" Phillip questioned. He certainly didn't want his arrival to cause an argument between Teddi and her father.

"Yes, Colonel Lane has been chaplain for the past five years. And a very fine one, I might add."

"Oh, I thought he was slated for retirement."

"You'll have to ask Father about that. I've heard nothing about his leaving. How is it that the army has assigned you as post surgeon *and* chaplain?"

"Guess they decided to make use of all my education. I applied for a transfer, hoping to become the chaplain, but the post surgeon position is the one that seemed to attract the most interest from my superiors. I was told that I would be able to fill both vacancies here," he replied. "But there are few other places outside of a church where one can minister as well as in a hospital."

"I don't see how you can possibly handle both positions. Not only does Chaplain Lane take care of his ministerial duties, but he also serves as librarian, and manager of House of Blazes No. 2."

"House of Blazes?"

"The post bakery," Teddi replied, obviously amazed he didn't know what she was talking about.

"There for a minute I thought you were referring to the afterlife. You know—those who don't get into heaven find themselves in the House of Blazes," he joked.

She merely gave him a weak smile and turned her attention back toward the passing scenery.

"Here we are, Officers' Row," Clayton announced as they came to a halt in front of a row of limestone officers' quarters.

Phillip spotted Mrs. Yorke watching from the parlor window as he offered his hand to assist Teddi out of the sleigh. He wondered if Mrs. Yorke knew why Teddi seemed so distant. The general obviously had no idea! Perhaps he would have an opportunity to speak privately with Mrs. Yorke before the afternoon was over.

"Here is my surprise," Teddi announced, quickly nodding

her head toward Phillip as the three of them walked through the front door. "You remember Phillip Hamilton, don't you, Mother?"

"Of course I do. It is absolutely wonderful to see you, Phillip. How are your parents? Doing well, I hope. Get out of those wraps and come into the dining room. Florence makes the best chicken and dumplings I've ever tasted, and she'll not soon forgive me if we let them get cold," she rattled without taking a breath.

"Do I take that to mean we are to join you in the dining room for our noonday meal, my dear?" the general asked with a glint in his eye.

"Well, of course," she replied, laughing at herself.

"My parents are doing very well and send their regards to all of you," Phillip answered, once they were seated in the dining room. "They were delighted that I would be serving under your command, General Yorke."

"I hope that one day Jonathan will have the privilege of serving under *your* father's command," Clayton replied. "You have fine parents. I've often wished that your father and I would be assigned to the same post once again."

"My father said the same thing when I told him of my assignment to Fort Riley," Phillip replied.

"How did you ever end up with this dual role as physician and chaplain?" Mrs. Yorke inquired after they'd given thanks for their meal. "I don't believe that I've ever heard of such a thing. Have *you*, my dear?" she asked as she offered Phillip a large tureen of fatback-seasoned green beans.

"Can't say as I have," Clayton replied, ladling a serving of the steaming chicken and dumplings onto his plate. "Smells wonderful, Florence," he complimented the maid, who was heading off toward the kitchen.

"Serving the Lord is *now* my first love. While attending medical school, I received God's call upon my life and knew that He wanted me to serve Him. I find that the two professions complement each other."

"So you feel the Lord wanted you to minister to our families and young men in the army! Well, I'm glad He's sent you to us. It's going to spread you a bit thin, having to serve in two positions, but you'll have Teddi to help you at the hospital. You couldn't ask for any better help than our Teddi. She's a fine nurse. You just ask any of those patients over in the hospital," General Yorke stated, nodding his head for emphasis.

"I don't doubt that. I'm looking forward to a close relationship with your daughter—*working* relationship, that is," he quickly added.

"If you'll excuse me, I've finished my meal and have some matters that need my attention upstairs," Teddi stated as she pushed away from the table.

"Teddi. . . ," Isabelle began.

"I'm sure you don't need me sitting here. You go ahead and catch up on old times," Teddi replied as she exited the room before anything further could be said.

Moments later, Florence scurried to the front door in answer to a resounding knock.

"General Yorke, you're needed back at headquarters for a staff meeting," the maid announced as she entered the dining room.

"Well, at least they waited until we had finished our meal. My apologies for running off, my boy, but I'm sure you understand. I'll be back at around three o'clock and show you to your quarters. I think you'll find the house more than adequate. If Teddi comes back downstairs, you might ask her to give you a tour of the hospital and chapel. I've left the sleigh tied outside," he suggested while he threw his military cloak around his shoulders and began walking toward the front door.

"Let's move to the parlor and have our coffee in there," Mrs. Yorke, ever the perfect hostess, suggested.

Phillip nodded in agreement, carried the tray and cups into the parlor, and then seated himself opposite the general's wife. "Mrs. Yorke, I believe I may have offended Teddi in some way. She seemed very displeased by my arrival. Can you tell me if there's something I've done—something she may have mentioned to you? We're going to be working together, and I certainly don't want us starting off on the wrong foot," Phillip explained.

"Perhaps you should ask Teddi," Isabelle tactfully suggested.

"I did, but she merely stated I'd done nothing to offend her since my arrival. If she's concerned about working with me, I want her to be assured that I'll do nothing to risk losing a fine nurse. What I mean to say is, I wouldn't be pursuing a romantic relationship with her."

Isabelle merely nodded at the last remark. She was relieved Teddi was upstairs, out of earshot. Phillip's quick assessment that he found Teddi undesirable as a romantic interest would only reinforce her daughter's belief that appearances were all that mattered to the opposite sex.

"Then I thought it might be something that occurred when we were youngsters. Perhaps some childhood prank? Can you help me?"

"What did you say? Some childish prank?" Isabelle questioned, obviously embarrassed that she hadn't been following Phillip's conversation.

"I wondered if Teddi might be upset about some childhood prank," Phillip repeated.

Isabelle leaned over and patted his hand. "I'm not sure exactly what is bothering Teddi, but I'm certain that when the time is right, she'll take you into her confidence."

three

Teddi sat staring at her reflection in the oval mirror that topped an oak chest in her bedroom. *It was just an insignificant childhood event that he doesn't even remember.* Yet that incident had been the cause of a great deal of pain throughout her growing years—it still caused her pain, or perhaps it was embarrassment. But if Phillip didn't even remember, there was no need to be embarrassed. And he *had* appeared truly baffled by the whole situation. Perhaps he couldn't recollect, or perhaps seeing that she had grown into what her mother called a somewhat *plain* young woman, he had no desire to remember her childish infatuation with him.

"Teddi, dear," her mother called from the bottom of the stairway. Teddi wanted to ignore the pleading tone in her mother's voice, but she couldn't. After all, her mother had nothing to do with Phillip Hamilton's reappearance in their lives.

"Yes, Mother?" Teddi responded, walking to face her mother from the top of the steps.

"Your father suggested that you take Phillip on a tour of the hospital and chapel. Do you feel up to doing that?"

"I'm not ill, Mother." The *last* thing Teddi wanted Phillip Hamilton to think was that his presence could so unnerve her that she would become physically ill. He would think her one of those fainthearted women who couldn't possibly be trusted to help run a hospital.

"Well, no, I realize you're not *ill*. But I didn't know if you wanted to go outdoors in this chilly weather," Isabelle replied, obviously wanting to give her daughter an excuse to remain at home if she so desired.

"I'll be down in just a moment. Tell Captain Hamilton that I'll escort him if *he* feels up to braving the snow and wind." Turning on her heel, she returned to the bedroom, ran a brush through her reddish brown hair, and then pulled the unruly locks into a cascade at the back of her head. Leaning in close to the mirror, she carefully checked her reflection. Puffy eyes would be a certain giveaway that she had been crying, and she wouldn't want Phillip Hamilton to think she would cry over some silly childhood occurrence. After patting her face with a cool cloth, she carefully applied a light dusting of powder under each eye. Checking the mirror one last time, she shook her head in disgust. Why did she even bother? No amount of powder was going to hide the size of her nose or cause her imperfect features to appear beautiful.

"Are you ready for your tour?" she asked as she entered the parlor a few minutes later.

"Absolutely! Whenever you are," Phillip answered as he bounded out of the collapsible Huntzinger chair in which he'd been seated. The piece of furniture folded and went crashing to the floor. "I'm sorry," he stammered as he sat the chair aright and then fumbled to replace the fringed tapestry cushion upon the seat.

Teddi grinned as she watched his attempts to rearrange the cushion. He had the fringe turned to the back of the chair instead of the front but hadn't yet discovered his error. When he turned toward her, she pointed to the chair. "I think that you need to turn the cushion—the fringe should be facing the front," she instructed.

"It's all right. I can fix that after you two have gone," Isabelle stated. "It happens to folks all the time, Phillip. Don't look so concerned."

"Mother! I don't remember that *ever* happening before," Teddi chastised. "You wouldn't be telling a fib to make the chaplain feel better, would you?"

"I most certainly would not!" her mother replied haughtily. "It's happened to your father several times, and you may feel free to inquire if that's not the truth. In fact, he now refuses to sit on a Huntzinger chair."

"I'm sorry, Mother. I should have known you wouldn't tell a lie—especially to someone as upstanding as Phillip," she said.

Seeing Phillip in a disconcerting situation seemed to relieve her anxiety. In fact, he appeared almost as uncomfortable as she was, and that thought gave her satisfaction.

"You want to drive the team or shall I?" Teddi asked as they reached the sleigh. The snow was no longer light and feathery but had turned to damp, heavy flakes that had accumulated to well over three inches of new snow.

"I will. You snuggle down under the blankets," he replied.

"It will be a little difficult to direct you if I'm in back under the blankets," Teddi responded. "I'll sit up front with you."

Phillip merely shrugged his shoulders. "Suit yourself—merely trying to be accommodating."

"No need. I'm capable of being out and about in the cold weather," Teddi replied.

"I'm sure you are," Phillip replied, a look of confusion crossing his face.

"Turn the horses to the right up here," she instructed, settling back on the seat.

Teddi loved Fort Riley and knew almost every inch of the grounds. Whenever they had visitors, Clayton was sure to take Teddi along on tours of the military post. She had become an accomplished guide, quick to point out every object of interest to anyone who would listen—but not on this trip. The sleigh coursed along down Soapsuds Row, the runners making a swooshing sound as they cut through the snow and carried them toward the post hospital.

"Is that it?" Phillip inquired, gesturing toward the sprawling, stone structure.

Teddi nodded. "That's it. There's a place out back where we can shelter the team and sleigh."

Phillip directed the horses toward the back of the two-story, limestone building. "It's larger than I expected," he commented as they walked under the covered porch that ran across the front and down the east side of the structure. To the west were the physician's quarters and the smaller quarters of the hospital steward. Beyond the porch, to the east, was what appeared to be a large, fenced garden. "Vegetable garden?"

"Yes, although the productivity this year was rather low. I didn't have enough time to tend to the garden and the patients. Sergeant Feighney offered to put some of the soldiers to work hoeing and pulling weeds, but reassigning the men from their regular duties to raise vegetables didn't seem proper—especially since Mr. and Mrs. Sawyer provide such excellent produce," Teddi replied as they entered the largest ward.

Several of the men pulled themselves to attention and saluted the captain as he walked toward them. "No need for that," Phillip said to one of the men as he struggled to salute. "This is a hospital, not the training field. I hear Miss Yorke has been giving you men fine care. You'll be sorry to hear that I've been assigned as the new post surgeon here at the fort, and I'll be relieving Miss Yorke of the extra duties she's been required to endure for the past four months."

Phillip was right. The men did appear sorry to hear the news. "You'll still be working here, won't you?" one of the young privates asked Teddi.

"Yes, I'll be assisting Dr. Hamilton and performing my nursing duties, although I doubt that I'll be seeing *you* much longer. Upon examination, I believe Dr. Hamilton will find you fit to return to duty," she replied, giving the soldier a broad smile.

"I'll miss seeing you, Miss Yorke, and that's a fact. But I

can't say I'll miss being cooped up in this hospital. You just say the word, Captain, and I'll be on my way," the private replied.

"I don't officially begin my duties until Monday. Think you can stand being hospitalized a few more days, or shall I have the hospital steward check you over?" Phillip inquired.

"I'll wait. I guess there's always the domino tournament to keep me busy."

"Interested in seeing the operating room?" Teddi asked when they left the ward and walked down a narrow hallway lined with wood-framed pictures of military officers in full-dress uniform.

"Absolutely," he replied, following her into a large room. A solitary, wooden operating table stood in the center of the stark-white, rectangular room. Oak cabinets and shelves containing instruments, medical supplies, and a variety of medical books lined the walls. "Instant reference for those operations that go awry?" he asked, nodding toward the books and giving her a chuckle.

She returned the laugh—with a soft, melodious intonation that appeared to stop him in his tracks. "Is something wrong?" she asked when he stood transfixed, staring at her.

"No, nothing—your laughter," he stammered.

"There's something wrong with my laugh?" she asked. He was tongue-tied, and she wasn't sure why. All she had done was laugh.

"No, you have a beautiful laugh. The sound reminds me of my mother's wind chimes—you know, that light, tinkling music they play when a soft breeze passes through on a summer day."

"I see. And it surprises you that someone that looks like me could have a pleasant laugh," Teddi responded as she nodded her head in understanding. "I shall consider your answer a compliment. Please accept my thanks, Phillip. Or do you prefer to be called 'Captain'?" she asked, adroitly changing the subject.

Phillip gave her a faint smile. "There was a time in my life when I would have *insisted* upon 'Captain.' Nowadays, military rank is of little importance to me. It's my position with the Lord that counts."

"Really? Perhaps that's an opinion you'd best keep to yourself when among some of the young officers who are busy working for those bars you're wearing."

"Quite the contrary, Teddi. I think they need to know that, ultimately, God is our commander in chief. Don't misunderstand—I feel that every soldier has an obligation to do his duty to the very best of his ability and serve his country proudly. But I also think we all need to keep God first in our lives—and that includes soldiers."

"Well put, Phillip. I stand corrected. Perhaps you *should* voice that opinion. It may not please some of the officers, but I'm sure your attitude pleases God," she replied, impressed with his remarks.

Teddi rode in silence as they traveled from the hospital to the old limestone chapel. She was thinking of Phillip's words. He had changed dramatically from the boy of seventeen that she remembered. Now, some ten years later, he was a man who had given his heart to the Lord. She was beginning to feel foolish for holding a grudge against him for something he'd done when he was still a schoolboy—something he obviously didn't even remember.

"That's the chapel up ahead," Teddi said, pointing toward the structure.

"Not many buildings made of wood on this post, are there?" Phillip asked as he drew the horses to a stop in front of the arched door of the stone building.

"A few. But limestone is prevalent in this area, and it can withstand just about anything. When the winds come whipping across the plains, I'd much rather be inside one of these stone buildings than in a frame house," she explained. "I don't know if Chaplain Lane is here. I didn't see his horse, but sometimes he walks. He lives in those quarters," she explained, pointing to a house at the end of a row not far from the church.

"Why don't you stay here, and I'll see if he's in the chapel. If not, we can get you back home. From the looks of the sky, it doesn't appear as if this snow will be letting up anytime soon. Can I assume this is the beginning of a long, hard winter in Kansas?"

"Not yet. We usually get one snowstorm at the end of October or early November. Then it lets up for a while, and we often don't see any more snow until December or January. But we do have bitterly cold winters in this part of the country, snow or no snow. When you stop at the sutler's store to purchase your supplies, you may want to consider investing in a buffalo coat. Most of the men living here find the warmth of a buffalo coat a necessity," she advised.

"I'll remember that," he said as he jumped down from the seat and ran up the steps to the chapel. "Door's locked," he called back to her.

She motioned him back to the sleigh. "Let's head home. Father is probably back at the house by now. I'm sure he'll want to introduce you to some of the other officers and give you a tour of your quarters. The surgeon's quarters are quite nice, although you may find them a bit large for only one person," she added.

"I hope I will have a wife and children to help fill my quarters one day," he replied.

"So you're engaged?" she ventured. *Why did I ask such a personal question? That will give him leave to do the same*, Teddi scolded herself.

"No, I'm not. I was engaged to a young lady once, but we've long since parted company. And you?"

I knew it! I left the door wide open for his questions, and he's walking right in, she thought. Giving him a smile, she folded her hands and placed them on her lap. "No, I have no plans for marriage. What happened to your young woman?" she inquired. *Oh, no! I've inquired into his personal life again,* she immediately thought. *I don't want to answer personal questions, but here I am barraging him with inquiries.* "I'm sorry; your past is *none* of my business. Please don't answer that question," she added quickly.

"I don't mind answering. After all, we're old friends, aren't we? I was engaged to a young lady whom I met while attending medical school. She was born into a Baltimore high-society family and was pleased with the idea of being married to a doctor and living in a large eastern city. She also thought that she could convince me to leave the army. Then when I decided to seek a position as a chaplain, she became furious—not enough prestige. That caused the final breach in our relationship. And I don't think she could picture herself living on military posts and never having a permanent home."

"Many women find the idea of military life unappealing, but once they've been subjected to the lifestyle, they make an admirable adjustment. I'm sure that your mother could have convinced her of the benefits."

"You're probably right—my mother has always enjoyed military life. But I decided that if Caroline was going to base her decision to marry me upon where we lived, perhaps she was more in love with the idea of marriage than with me. The last I heard, she was happily married to a bank president. I'm sure she's very content. And what of yourself? Surely you've had opportunity to tie the knot or break some fellow's heart."

"I tend to shy away from discussing my personal life," she replied as they reached home. "There's Father," she continued while pointing toward the general, who was sitting atop a chestnut mare and heading in their direction.

four

Teddi's answer was so serious. She obviously felt that he had crossed the boundaries of etiquette with his brazen questions about marriage proposals. Phillip certainly didn't want to frighten her off. If there was one thing he knew, it was that he needed Teddi's capable assistance at the hospital.

"I'm sorry, sir. What did you say?" Phillip stammered. The general was standing beside him with a look of amusement on his face.

"Finding your new duty assignment a bit overwhelming?" General Yorke inquired as he slapped Phillip on the back and gave him a hearty laugh, which caused a frosty white puff of vapor to hang in the freezing afternoon air. "I merely asked if Teddi had given you the grand tour of Fort Riley."

"No, just the hospital and chapel. She seemed a bit chilled," Phillip replied as the two men entered the house.

"Never thought I'd see the day Teddi Yorke would give up a chance to talk about the marvels of this military post. She usually bridles visitors and forces them to listen to every minute detail," the general stated while stomping the remaining snow off his boots.

"Careful with the mess you're making in that hallway, Clayton. I don't think you're ever going to remember to come in the back entrance when you're covered with snow or mud," Isabelle chastised her husband as she bustled toward the front door.

"You mean we have a back door to these quarters?" Clayton asked, placing a hand alongside his cheek and feigning surprise.

31

"Oh, Clayton! That's not the least bit funny," Isabelle remarked, her eyes cast downward toward the snow that was beginning to puddle around her husband's feet.

"I thought that's why you put this old piece of carpet on top of the good one," the general continued, oblivious to his wife's exasperated glance.

"I put that ugly, old rug down because you won't follow instructions," Isabelle replied, though unable to suppress a smile.

"Phillip and I thought we'd join you ladies for some hot tea or cocoa, whichever you prefer," Clayton stated as he hung his cloak on one of the wooden pegs.

"Where's Teddi?" Phillip asked, surveying the room.

"I believe she's gone upstairs to her room," Isabelle answered, a slight blush coloring her cheeks. "I'll see to some refreshments and be back in just a few moments."

Phillip's gaze rested upon the box-style grand piano sitting along the west wall of the parlor. He could recall Teddi sitting on the velvet-cushioned stool as a young girl, her fingers running over the ivory keys as she practiced to the rhythm of the clicking metronome.

"I don't know what's gotten into that girl today. She's not acting like herself," General Yorke mused as he joined Phillip.

"Perhaps she doesn't find my company very appealing," Phillip ventured. "I fear I'm the cause of her unusual behavior. I'm sure that it has something to do with our younger days at Fort McHenry, but for the life of me, I can't remember what I did, *or didn't do*, that has offended her. Do you have any idea what the problem may be?"

"How could you be a problem? Teddi was a mere child when the two of you last saw each other—she would have been only twelve or thirteen, at most. No, I think her mood has more to do with Captain Albright than with you, Phillip."

Before Phillip had an opportunity to explore who Captain Albright was and what that man might have to do with Teddi's behavior, Isabelle returned with a tray bearing her etched silver teapot, cups, saucers, and a plate heaped with buttery, fresh-baked cookies.

"So that's why it smells so good in here! Florence has been baking again. I do enjoy that woman's culinary abilities—not that you can't put her to shame, my dear," Clayton quickly added.

"Ever the diplomat," Isabelle replied, giving him a broad smile as she poured the steaming liquid into three cups. "Sugar?" she asked, meeting Phillip's gaze.

"No, plain is fine," he replied. "Perhaps Teddi would care to join us?" he optimistically inquired.

"Oh, I don't think. . ."

"Phillip fears he's done something to offend our Teddi," the general explained, interrupting his wife, "but I told him I was sure that her mood had more to do with Herbert Albright's antics than anything Phillip might have done years ago."

"Clayton!"

"What? Did I say something wrong?" he asked, a bewildered look crossing his face.

"I don't think Teddi would appreciate your discussing her broken engagement to Captain Albright," Isabelle chided.

"I didn't discuss it. In fact, I didn't even tell him she had been engaged. All I said was. . ."

"Goodness! Now look what I've done with my jabbering. Teddi will never forgive me."

"Forgive you for what, Mother?" Teddi asked as she gracefully entered the room and seated herself in a wicker chair opposite her father.

"How about one of Florence's famous butter cookies?" the general asked, extending the plate toward his daughter.

Teddi shook her head. "No, I don't care for anything to eat

right now. What were. . ."

"Tea then?" the general interrupted. "Pour her a cup of tea, Isabelle. I'm sure she'd like that."

"Yes, of course," Isabelle replied while quickly turning her attention toward the tray.

"Tell me, Phillip, what did you think of our hospital?" the general inquired, obviously intent on ignoring Teddi's earlier question.

"I was *very* impressed. And the patients reacted much as you'd anticipated—none of them wanted a replacement for Teddi. As far as I could tell, the men are more than pleased with the care they've been receiving. And I'm sure their assessment is warranted. I doubt that any of them could have received better care anywhere."

He turned toward Teddi with a smile on his face. But she didn't smile in return. Instead, there was a look he couldn't quite comprehend. Not anger, but that look certainly couldn't be mistaken for joy, either. Irritation. That was it! She had a distinct look of irritation—and that look was aimed directly toward him. But why? He hadn't done or said anything inappropriate. It was her parents who were dropping hints about some past affair of the heart and a Captain Albright. So why didn't she aim her looks of disdain toward them instead of him?

"Yes, she's gained quite an excellent reputation among the medical community as well," Isabelle chimed in. "When Dr. Jeffries was the post surgeon, he couldn't say enough good things about Teddi. In fact, Dr. Jeffries is now out of the military and has a flourishing medical practice in Junction City. Would you believe that rascal tried to convince Teddi to quit her work at the hospital and come to work for him?"

"I wouldn't have *any* problem believing that, Mrs. Yorke," Phillip replied. He didn't turn to look toward Teddi, fearful he'd be met by another one of her frowning stares. "Perhaps

I should think about getting settled into my quarters," Phillip continued as he handed his cup and saucer to Mrs. Yorke.

"There's no need to hurry. In fact, why don't you spend the night with us? We have plenty of room, and it's already beginning to turn dark outside. These fall days are so short. Besides, you'll have ample time to get settled over the next few days, won't he, Clayton?" Isabelle asked. "Don't you think it's best if Phillip spends the night with us?"

"Yes, of course! We'll not hear of you leaving us so soon. If I weren't concerned that a few eyebrows might be raised, I'd insist on your living with us while you're stationed here. Having you in the house would almost be like having Jonathan home again," Clayton replied.

"Father! Having a stranger in the house is *nothing* like having Jonathan with us," Teddi retorted.

"Phillip isn't a stranger, Teddi. With this nomadic life we lead, he's about as close to family as we could hope for," the general replied, his voice tinged with displeasure.

"I'm sorry, Father," Teddi replied with a note of contrition in her voice.

"I don't want to be any trouble. . . ."

"You'll be no trouble at all, and tomorrow we can get you settled in your own place, Phillip," Isabelle interrupted as she gave her daughter a sidelong glance.

"Take your bags and follow Isabelle upstairs. She'll show you to your room," Clayton said as he rose from his chair and gave Phillip a smile. "Teddi, why don't you join me in the kitchen?"

❧

At the very least, Teddi knew that she owed her father respect and obedience—and she was sure that she was going to be told those very words once she was alone with him. Clayton Yorke wouldn't consider the fact that Teddi disliked the comparison of Phillip Hamilton and her brother Jonathan. There were certain behaviors the Yorkes would not tolerate, and one of them was rudeness—especially from one of their children. It was obvious that she had provoked her parents, and the meager apology she had offered would do little to salve her father's displeasure. She should apologize to Phillip, but she wasn't up to making amends just now. Besides, any excuse she could make would ring false. *No apology is better than a contrived one, isn't that true?* she rationalized.

Her father wasn't about to waste time dealing with her boorish behavior. His jaw was firmly set and his shoulders squared as he led the way through the parlor and back toward the kitchen. Teddi had barely set foot in the room when her father pivoted on his heel and faced her. His normally ruddy complexion had turned the purplish red shade of a freshly picked beet, and his dark brown eyes shone with anger.

"Would you like to explain what has gotten into you? I can't believe that a child of mine would treat another human being so impolitely. *Well?* What do you have to say for yourself?"

"I'm sorry, Father. You're right, of course, but your comparison of Phillip and Jonathan caught me off guard—I lost my sense of good judgment. My behavior was terribly rude. I'm sorry; I totally forgot my manners. *Please* accept my apology," she implored.

"It's Phillip to whom you owe an apology. Can you imagine how embarrassing that whole scene must have been for him? Just put yourself in his place for a moment. And it's not merely that insult you threw in his direction—you've been ungracious to him ever since he set foot in the train station. He asked me earlier what he'd done to offend you."

"What did you tell him?" Teddi pleaded.

"I told him that I didn't see how he could have done anything—especially since he hasn't seen you for all these years."

"Is that *all* you said?"

"No," Clayton hesitated a moment. "I told him that I thought your attitude had more to do with Captain Albright than with him."

"You didn't!"

"I did. At that particular moment, I thought I was making a true statement. Now I'm not so sure."

"How *could* you, Father?"

"How could I *what?* Tell him that I thought he was blameless? Because that's what I believe," Clayton replied.

"No! How could you tell a complete stranger that Herbert had broken our engagement? It's none of Phillip's business. It's nobody's business."

"I didn't tell him about your broken engagement. Your mother did that!"

Teddi fell onto one of the wooden kitchen chairs with a plop. Everything was swirling about. None of this made any sense. She felt her cheeks grow warm and glanced toward the hearth, where flames licked upward and radiated heat throughout the room. It took a moment for Teddi to gain her composure. But then the full impact of her father's words struck home.

"What? Mother wouldn't—she *couldn't* have done anything as thoughtless and cruel as to tell that, that. . ."

"Old friend?"

"That *stranger*. . ."

"Thou doth protest too much, my dear. I think there's more here than meets the eye."

"I don't care to discuss anything except why Mother felt inclined to betray my confidence."

"She felt no such inclination. She thought that I had already told Phillip about your broken engagement. Your mother was in the process of reprimanding me for what she considered a violation of your privacy. Little did she realize that she was providing Phillip with information he'd not heard from my lips. Unfortunately, we made a mistake. Quite frankly, I don't think Phillip is going to use the information to do you any harm," her father replied in an obvious attempt to make light of the situation.

"This *isn't* amusing. My personal life is none of Phillip Hamilton's business. He's the last person I would *ever* trust."

"Why don't you tell me what this is *really* about, Teddi?"

Her voice was no more than a whisper as she croaked out a tearful reply. "It's about betrayal, Father. Now, if you'll excuse me, I have nothing further to say." She turned and ran up the back stairway that led from the kitchen to the rear hallway of the second floor.

She knew that she was overreacting, allowing her behavior to be clouded by the anger and frustration of her broken engagement to Herbert. But the wound was still fresh, an embarrassment inflicted upon her in front of both the military and civilian communities. Tongues had wagged incessantly when her engagement to Herbert had been announced. Herbert Albright, the strikingly handsome, young captain, interested in marrying the homely Teddi Yorke? She knew the stories that had circulated soon after the announcement— tales of Herbert's desire to enhance his chances of being promoted through the ranks of the military by marrying the general's daughter. After all, they surmised, why else would he be interested in marrying unattractive Teddi?

Only months later, the rumormongers had new grist for their gossip mill. Herbert had broken his engagement to Teddi, pledged his undying love to a young debutante in Junction City, and planned to marry her in December. The marriage, however, had been hastened when Herbert received military orders sending him to Fort Brown. It had given Teddi some sense of relief to know that she wouldn't be forced to socialize with Herbert and his fiancée. And although Herbert's departure had helped to subdue the gossip, Teddi still received more than a few pitying looks as she entered a room or walked about town.

Reaching the top of the stairway in record time, she rounded the corner and, with a resounding thud, collided headlong into Phillip Hamilton's broad chest. Teddi watched the satchels drop from his hands and hit the floor. In one fluid movement, his arms raised and he grasped her by the shoulders.

"I can't seem to stay out of your way," he whispered, their eyes only inches apart.

"It's my fault. I wasn't watching where I was going. I'm sorry for my rude behavior. Please accept my apology."

"Apology accepted," Phillip replied.

His voice was barely audible, and Teddi leaned closer as he spoke. She heard him accept her apology, but it sounded as though he had added something else. She looked at his mouth, but it wasn't moving. Perhaps she was hearing things. Allowing herself another glimpse, she stared at his unmoving lips and then permitted her eyes to travel upward until she met Phillip's questioning gaze. Startled, she jumped back, freeing herself from his grasp.

"Any chance that we could start over and become friends again?" Phillip ventured.

"I don't know. I really don't know, Phillip," she stammered.

Making her way around him, she hastily proceeded down the hall and into her bedroom. Closing the door behind her, she clutched the doorknob in her hand and leaned her forehead against the dark, cool wood. What was happening to her? She had vowed never to have feelings for another man, especially a handsome man who was bound to cause her nothing but heartache.

five

December 1870

"Hurry, Mother! They're here."

Isabelle Yorke pulled off the muslin apron that had carefully protected her green, lace-trimmed dress throughout the last-minute preparations for her children. Her face was flushed with excitement, and the rigors of assuring that the house was in perfect order had added a becoming blush to her already pink cheeks. Rushing to the front door, she came to a halt just as Jonathan and George, the youngest of her four sons, bounded onto the front porch, immediately followed by their father.

"Stomp that snow off your feet before you come in here," she ordered.

"Listen to *her*, George! We haven't even received a welcoming hug, and she's reminding us about the house rules." Jonathan stomped his feet wildly and watched as his mother shook her finger in mock indignation. "Come here, Mother," he ordered, playfully grabbing Isabelle and twirling her around before setting her back on her feet. "You look grand! And *you*," he said while pulling his sister into an embrace, "look magnificent. Doesn't she, George?"

"You both need to get inside so I can close the front door, or I'm going to be in your mother's bad graces for the rest of the day," Clayton said as he pushed the boys forward. "Surely you both remember. . ."

"We don't live in a barn," they both chimed in unison.

"I can see this is going to be one of those make-fun-of-Mother's-rules days. That's perfectly fine with me. It's those

40

rules that have turned both of you into fine, upstanding young men who will one day be commendable husbands. And, I might add, I would like to think that a marriage might occur within the near future? Grandchildren would be lovely," she merrily gibed in return.

"You can't make us feel guilty about our bachelorhood, Mother. You already have four grandchildren. William and Martin have taken care of that request," George quickly replied.

"That's true, but one can never have enough grandchildren. Besides, I seldom get to see any of them."

"It would seem that if you want grandchildren close at hand, you should be pushing Teddi toward the altar, not us," Jonathan retorted while giving his sister a wink.

Teddi cringed at the remark, but said nothing.

"Speaking of which, I can't understand how you've escaped marriage while living among all the lonely men on a military post," George added.

"Remaining single hasn't been so difficult. Men can be afflicted by a wandering eye, even when there's a shortage of women," Teddi responded with a weak smile. "Anyway, things aren't as bleak as you might suspect. We have more social activities than you might expect, and there are quite a number of single, young ladies in Junction City who are included in our gatherings. So, you see, these men aren't overly deprived."

"No single young men live in Junction City?" Jonathan inquired.

"Of course. And they're included also, but I didn't want George thinking that there were no women to be found in Kansas. In fact, I'd be pleased to introduce both of you to several young ladies. I'm sure the holiday festivities will be greatly enhanced with a suitable lady on your arm."

"That's most kind of you, Teddi. I may take you up on the offer," George replied. "Speaking of festivities, I was hoping for some of your delicious molasses cookies before waiting much longer, Mother."

"Only the *molasses* cookies?" Isabelle called from the kitchen. "As I recall, you never had a preference, as long as they were sweet and piled high on the plate."

George laughed as he rose from the velvet-cushioned rocking chair. "That would be correct, Mother. Would you like me to help you? I can fix a plate for myself out there in the kitchen. That would save you from running back and forth to replenish the supply for everyone else."

"Some things never change," Isabelle remarked as she entered the dining room carrying a two-tiered silver serving tray laden with an appealing array of cookies. Florence followed close behind, balancing the tea service and a platter heaped with thick slices of fruitcake, while George rubbed his hands together and circled the table for a better view.

"Now *this* is what I call hospitality," George announced after completing his inspection of the pastries. "I do miss home cooking. Perhaps Florence would like to come live back East and become *my* housekeeper?"

"You know better than that, Mister George. I like working for your mama and papa just fine. You single boys are just too messy," Florence joked as she scurried back to the kitchen.

Wagging her finger at George, Isabelle furrowed her eyebrows and gave him a frown.

"What? It was worth a try, wasn't it?" George questioned.

"I've worked my fingers to the bone, baking and cleaning for you boys, hoping for the best holiday in years. And what are my thanks? You come into the house and try to steal away the best cook this side of the Mississippi!" Isabelle replied, feigning indignation.

"Now, Mother, you know I would never take Florence away from you," George answered as he continued piling cookies on his plate.

"You can go back for seconds, George. You don't need to pile those so high that they end up on the floor. We're going to think you haven't had anything to eat since you left Washington," Clayton said with a laugh.

"We've eaten, Father. It's just that growing boys are hard to keep full," George answered.

"Speak for yourself, George. I consider myself a man," Jonathan called out, his comment causing the room to fill with laughter.

"You folks sit still; I'll get it," Florence instructed as she rushed through the dining room in response to a sharp knock at the front door.

"I hope that's not Sergeant Luckert wanting to pull me away from my family," Clayton commented while carefully choosing several cookies.

"Look what the wind blew in," Florence announced. She was holding onto Phillip's arm while pulling him forward into the dining room. Meanwhile, Phillip was glancing back behind himself, obviously unsure whether he was tracking snow into the house.

The entire family rose to greet Phillip, with each voice attempting to rise above the other in a hearty welcome to their newly arrived guest. The entire family with the exception of Teddi, that is. She alone remained seated and mute, observing the familial scene as though she were no longer a member of the group. However, no one seemed to notice. No one except Phillip, who met her glance and gave her what appeared to be a questioning expression in return.

"Sit down, sit down," Jonathan urged his friend, pulling a chair up beside his own and patting the seat. "I must tell you, Phillip, the fact that you're here at Fort Riley made it impossible for me to stay away this Christmas. The opportunity to see both my family and my closest friend all at the same time—how could I possibly turn down such an occasion?

How have you been? Is Father making your life unbearable? No, I'd wager it's my sister who's truly making life unbearable. I can't imagine how you put up with our little Teddi all day long at the hospital. Tell me, what's your secret for getting along with our little sister?"

Phillip squirmed in his chair for a moment as all eyes rested upon him, mischievous smiles lurking upon their lips in anticipation of his forthcoming answer. Teddi merely stared at him, her eyes void of expression. There wasn't a hint of amusement on her face as she waited along with the others to hear what he might say.

"Actually, she makes it quite easy. Whenever I enter a room, she finds an excuse to leave," Phillip finally replied.

"But that can't work for long. How do you take care of patients without talking to her?" Jonathan persisted.

"Your sister prefers written instructions rather than verbal," Phillip answered. "So tell me, Jonathan, how are you enjoying your assignment?"

"He's trying to change the subject and thinks I won't notice," Jonathan told his family. "I'm enjoying it immensely, though probably not as much as you're enjoying Fort Riley. Teddi tells me there are flocks of beautiful young women in these parts and numerous social activities. Have you found yourself someone special—aside from our Teddi, that is?"

"No, no one. Aside from Teddi, as you put it."

"And what of the social happenings? Are they as exciting as our sister boasts?"

"I couldn't answer that. I've attended only a few," Phillip responded.

"But he's taking part in the theater production, which will debut next week," Isabelle offered.

"So you're putting your thespian abilities to good use. I'm glad to hear that. He was quite the actor while we were in school. Several of the instructors encouraged him to consider studying abroad and make acting his career choice," Jonathan told his family.

"Well, I, for one, am glad he didn't. He's a remarkable asset to the army," Clayton replied.

"I never gave acting any serious consideration. My father would have throttled me," Phillip remarked.

"I must say I'm surprised to hear there's a theater out here in the Wild West. Are you hoping to completely civilize your troops, Father?" George joked.

"Now, don't you start looking down your nose at the military, young man. We're every bit as cultured as you Easterners," Isabelle warned.

"Watch out, George. You're going to get Mother on her soapbox if you keep it up," Jonathan teased.

"I'll have you both know that we have a grand theatrical hall. It's been completed only this past year, and you two will be privileged to see the first major production," Isabelle replied as she began clearing dishes from the table. "Why don't you go into the parlor, and I'll join you shortly."

"I'll help, Mother," Teddi offered, but Isabelle shook her head and waved the group away from the table and into the adjoining room.

Teddi remained at the table a few moments, hoping that perhaps she could escape up the back stairway to her room. After spending the past month anticipating her brothers' arrival, she now disliked the idea of sharing them with Phillip. It was obvious her mother had invited him, and just as obvious that her mother had intentionally failed to include Teddi in that decision. As far as Teddi was concerned, Isabelle had been Phillip's strongest supporter since his arrival. She included him for Sunday dinners, seated him beside Teddi at the military ball, assured his name was included on invitation lists for the Junction City social gatherings, and even took warm meals to him when she knew he was working late at the hospital. However, when Teddi complained to her father, he laughed and said Isabelle was merely enjoying having a boy around to take care of once again.

"Come on, Teddi," Jonathan called, breaking into her thoughts. "Fill us in on this theater and the play that will be presented. I'm sure you have a starring role."

Teddi stood in the doorway to the parlor, glanced around the room, and then shrunk back. The only remaining seats were her mother's rocker, which Teddi wouldn't dare occupy, and the sofa, where Phillip was already seated.

"Come have a seat," Phillip urged, nodding toward the empty space beside him.

"Better yet, why don't we go see the theatrical hall?" Teddi suggested. "They just finished hanging the new drop curtain last night after we completed practice. I haven't even had an opportunity to see it."

The four men glanced at each other, obviously content to stay and enjoy their full stomachs and the warmth exuding from the glowing fireplace.

"Why don't you young people go? I'll stay here and keep Isabelle company," Clayton suggested as he wriggled down into his chair a little farther.

"Come on. Don't be so lazy, you two," Teddi urged as she poked her finger first in one brother's chest and then the other's.

"I don't suppose she'll give us a moment's peace unless we accompany her," George said, eyeing Jonathan and Phillip.

"Guess we might as well give in," Jonathan agreed while rising from his chair. "Come on, Phillip. I'm not going to let you stay here and keep warm while we go traipsing about the post."

"He doesn't *have* to come," Teddi responded just as Phillip stood up.

The room fell silent, and nobody moved for a moment.

"Unless he truly wants to," Teddi quickly added.

It was a halfhearted attempt to restore a bit of decorum to the uncomfortable situation she'd created, but it was the best she could muster at the moment. Phillip wasn't *really* welcome, at least not where she was concerned. These were her brothers, and she didn't want to share them, especially with someone as disquieting as Phillip Hamilton.

"Of course he wants to. And *I* want him to," Jonathan responded, giving his sister a surprised look.

The group was unusually quiet as the foursome made their way to the building, but the silence was soon broken when Phillip announced their arrival. "There it is," he said, pointing toward the long frame building.

"Well, I must admit, I'm surprised. The building must be at least 120 feet long," George commented.

"One hundred and thirty-five," Phillip answered.

"And sixty-eight feet wide," Teddi added. "Wait until you see the stage. It's huge. And the auditorium will seat eight hundred people," she exclaimed as they entered the building.

"And would you look at that curtain," Jonathan remarked, walking toward the stage.

"It's beautiful," Teddi replied as she gazed at the skillful touch the artist had rendered upon the curtain. "Even the folds of the drapery can't be seen."

"Looks like the Bay of Naples with Mt. Vesuvius in the distance," George replied.

"Who's the artist?" Jonathan inquired.

"One of the soldiers," Phillip answered.

"I'd say he's missed his true calling. And speaking of callings, Phillip, how is your ministry going? Are you able to spend time gathering a flock, or are you too busy taking care of their medical maladies?"

"I haven't been able to spend as much time as I'd like, but it's working out. The previous post chaplain, Colonel Lane, retired only a few weeks ago, giving me adequate time in which to acquaint myself with the medical part of my position before beginning my work with the spiritual side. I'm hoping to implement a few new ideas, but mostly I'll follow Colonel Lane's lead."

"What new ideas?" Teddi questioned. "You think there are things you can add that would make the chapel better than when Colonel Lane was in charge?"

Phillip hesitated for a moment. "No, not better," he cautiously answered. "Just add a little more variety. Change is good for the soul, don't you think?"

"Absolutely," Jonathan enthusiastically responded, while slapping his friend on the back.

"I see no need for change when things are going as well as they are," Teddi countered.

"I'm not really changing much, Teddi. I thought it might be nice to have a candlelight Christmas Eve service. Colonel Lane said he had never done that. I also thought it might be nice to have a Sunday school class for married couples to attend together instead of going to a men's or women's class. These are merely ideas; nothing's been decided. Colonel Lane suggested I change things a bit, breathe fresh life into the body of believers. You know, stir things up a little," Phillip added.

Teddi remained silent. How could she argue if Colonel Lane had given Phillip the go-ahead to promote change? To make matters more difficult, his ideas sounded quite innovative and exciting, but that didn't mean she had to like them. Since he had assumed his new duties, there'd been nothing but change going on in her life. In particular, Captain Hamilton had managed to stir up emotions and feelings that Teddi wasn't ready to deal with.

six

As he sat in one of the leather-upholstered chairs in Phillip's office the next morning, Jonathan was puzzled about why Phillip had insisted they meet so early in the day. After all, he was on leave and enjoyed sleeping a little later than usual, and he was certain his mother had invited Phillip to dinner that evening. Consequently, there seemed to be no logical reason for this meeting. Jonathan couldn't think of anything Phillip might want to discuss that couldn't have been better said as they relaxed with coffee in the parlor after a satisfying evening meal. But Phillip had been insistent, and Jonathan had relented.

Now, after waiting for fifteen minutes, he was becoming irritable and even more certain that this meeting could have waited until a civil time of day. Jumping up from his chair, he paced the length of the room several times and then wandered to a bookshelf that lined the west wall of the room. Running his fingers across the leather-bound volumes, he finally pulled one of the books from the shelf, flipped back the cover, glanced through several pages, and shoved it back onto the shelf with a grunt of disgust.

"Looks like Greek to me," he mumbled, looking at another one of the volumes.

"Actually, it's Hebrew," Phillip replied, striding into the office. "Sorry to keep you waiting. Had an unexpected patient show up."

"You should have left the patient to Teddi. She loves taking care of emergencies," Jonathan said with a chuckle.

"I give Teddi only those duties she's been accustomed to handling or the ones she volunteers to complete. Besides, it's a bit early, and she hasn't yet arrived at the hospital. In fact, that's why I asked you to come here for our talk. I wanted it to be private—just the two of us. We could have met at my quarters, but it would have appeared rude for me to invite you and not include George."

"Believe me, George wouldn't have even considered getting out at this time of day when he's on holiday. What's so private that you can't mention it in front of anyone else?" Jonathan asked, his interest obviously piqued.

"Teddi," Phillip simply stated.

"Teddi? What about her?"

"I've done something that has angered her. Unfortunately, I can't get her to tell me what it is, so I don't know how to make amends."

"You've been here only a couple of months, Phillip. How could you possibly have managed to mess things up so badly in that short a time?" Jonathan joked.

"No, it's not since I've been here. Something in the past, before I ever arrived," Phillip replied.

"How can that be?"

"I'm hoping you can tell me," Phillip answered.

For the next hour, Phillip related the events that had transpired since his arrival: Teddi's obvious disapproval of him because of something he'd supposedly done to hurt her in the past; her anger that Isabelle had mentioned Teddi's broken engagement; and her obvious distrust of men, particularly him.

"I even went so far as to ask your mother what I'd done. But she wasn't of any assistance. Can you give me any help with this, Jonathan? I'm at a complete loss."

"You haven't seen Teddi since you moved from Fort McHenry, have you?" Jonathan quizzed.

"No, that's not possible."

Jonathan eyed his friend. "Do you have feelings for Teddi?"

"I have the highest regard for her. She's an excellent nurse, has a quick wit, and is intelligent, capable, compassionate, and devout in her religious beliefs. . . ," Phillip hedged.

"But she doesn't possess the beauty necessary to make you a good wife," Jonathan interrupted.

"That's unfair, Jonathan. I recall that *you* always look for the most attractive young lady with a comely figure when you're seeking out prospective love interests," Phillip countered.

"I suppose that *is* true enough. It's just that, to me, Teddi is beautiful. She's the most engaging woman I know. She can discuss almost any subject with as much authority and intelligence as a man, while at the same time, she finds pleasure in decorating a home or teaching small children. And how could I think her anything but handsome? People say we look like twins," Jonathan added.

Phillip shifted in his chair. He knew that Jonathan's statements were true. A person's outer appearance was not a true measure of who that person was. And he genuinely liked Teddi's company, working side by side with her in the hospital, especially on those occasions when she let down her guard and didn't measure every word that she said. But his feelings for her stopped short of romance.

"For now, I want to be Teddi's friend, but there is something that's preventing her from trusting me. I need to find out what that is, and I'm hoping you can help," Phillip finally replied.

"Let's think back to when you left Fort McHenry," Jonathan suggested, falling silent for a moment. "Teddi was infatuated with you—remember? In fact, she gave you that silver sleigh bell that my father had special-ordered for her charm bracelet. Oh, boy, did she ever get into trouble for that," Jonathan recalled, putting his hand alongside his face and letting out a howl. "Father was furious. Teddi was in trouble the rest of the summer."

"She can't still be angry about that," Phillip protested. "I told her that I didn't want to take her sleigh bell, but she insisted. Besides, I gave it to you to return to her. You *did* return it to her, didn't you?" Phillip persisted.

Jonathan's face turned ashen. He looked as though he were going to be sick.

"Are you all right?" Phillip asked, moving toward his friend.

Jonathan nodded his head. "I think so, but you may never speak to me again."

"Why?"

"I completely forgot about the sleigh bell. I never gave it back to Teddi. After you gave it to me, I put it in a small wooden box in the bottom of my bureau drawer for safe-keeping until I returned home from college. I've never taken it out of the bureau," Jonathan admitted.

Phillip folded his hands and sat on the edge of the desk across from his friend. "I see. I suppose she has a right to be angry with me," Phillip murmured.

"Perhaps. But I think this has more to do with her broken engagement than the return of that charm," Jonathan argued.

"Perhaps it's a combination of things. She felt betrayed by me when she was young because I never answered her letters and didn't return her valuable gift. Then, only weeks before I reenter her life, she's betrayed by her fiancé. My presence serves only to reaffirm those feelings of betrayal. The problem is now compounded by the fact that if you return the sleigh bell, she'll never believe I gave it back to you years ago. I'm certain that she'll think I've put you up to it," Phillip finished with a sigh.

"If I try to talk to her about what's going on in her life, ask her why she's behaving so rudely toward you, it will present an opening. If she mentions the sleigh bell, I can tell her I have it and explain that you asked me to return it long ago. The truth is, I *have* wondered why she is so inhospitable to you. I thought perhaps she was romantically interested in you but you had rebuffed her," Jonathan remarked discreetly.

"She's given no indication that she has any interest in me. In fact, I think she wishes I'd never arrived at Fort Riley. Attempting to figure out why has just about driven me mad," Phillip emphatically replied.

Jonathan laughed. "My sister has a knack for driving even the soundest mind into turmoil, it seems."

"I've not given into it quite yet," Phillip replied. "But if I don't figure out how to win her trust and become her friend in the foreseeable future, you may have to commit me to the nearest asylum," he said, joining Jonathan's laughter.

"I'll talk to her and see if I can somehow help untangle this mess that I'm afraid I've helped to create," Jonathan promised as the two of them left the chapel. "You are coming over for dinner tonight?"

"Yes, but we have dress rehearsal this evening. Why don't you come along? I'm merely an understudy. We can sit in the audience and watch the performance," Phillip suggested.

"I'll see what mother has planned. I've promised to haul boxes of Christmas decorations from the storage room. She wants to go through the old ornaments and discard the ragged things. Of course, she'll end up keeping it all. She can't ever bring herself to throw away those ugly little decorations we've all made for her throughout the years."

Phillip nodded and laughed. "I know. My mother is the same way."

❧

Teddi sat in the meager dressing room while rehearsing her lines one last time. Above all else, she needed to remain calm. The last thing she wanted to do was go on stage and deliver her lines in a warbling voice. There was still an hour before the curtain would go up, but she could already hear the excited voices of theater patrons as they arrived. Last night's dress rehearsal had gone smoothly. Corporal Wigand had forgotten his line in one place, but she'd been able to prompt him without anyone noticing. Even the director hadn't caught on, and the play had continued without further mishap. She hoped things would go as well this evening.

The orchestra was beginning to warm up, and the tentative sounds of violins strumming and horns tooting in preparation for the overture sifted through the door. Teddi relaxed, knowing that soon the conglomeration of sounds would blend together in beautiful harmony.

"Change in cast, Miss Yorke," Private Mosier announced after lightly tapping on her door.

"Who? Why?" Teddi asked, yanking open the door and meeting the young private eye to eye.

"Corporal Wigand is ill. Terrible case of laryngitis—nothing but croaking noises," the private explained while pointing to his own throat. "Captain Hamilton, his understudy, will play the part."

"Phillip Hamilton is going to play the lead opposite me?" Teddi asked, her mouth gaping open in surprise.

"He's the only understudy we have for that part," the private replied with a quizzical expression.

"Of course. Captain Hamilton will be playing the part. Thank you, private," Teddi replied as she closed the door, made her way back across the room, and fell into the straight-backed wooden chair. *Phillip is playing the lead. We haven't even practiced together. How could this happen?* she wondered. The director had been so certain there would be no need for understudies, he'd never even bothered to check and see if any of them knew their lines.

Quickly she made her way down the hall and stopped in front of Corporal Wigand's dressing room. She hesitated only a moment and then lightly tapped on the door. "Phillip, it's Teddi. Are you in there?"

"Yes," he replied from the other side. "I've not finished

dressing, so I don't think I'd better open the door."

"Of course not! I just wanted to ask if you've memorized your part. Since the understudies have never practiced, I just wanted to assure myself. . ."

"I'll do my best to keep from embarrassing you," he interrupted.

"It's not me that I'm worried about," she began.

"Oh, really? You were worried about *me?*" he asked, pulling open the door and meeting her gaze.

"Well, yes," she stammered. "You and the others in the play. We've worked so hard, and. . ."

"I know that you've worked hard, Teddi. But this is only a few hours of entertainment, a means of amusing those in attendance. If we forget a word or two and give them cause for laughter, that's all right, too, don't you think?"

"No, at least not for me. We've all worked too hard to be laughed at. This isn't a comedy. Furthermore, it will be yet another embarrassment for me to endure. Now, do you know the lines or don't you?" Teddi insisted.

"Yes, Teddi, I know the lines," Phillip replied and promptly closed the door, leaving her staring at the wobbling cardboard placard that had been stenciled with Gardner Wigand's name.

Turning on her heel, she marched down the hall, entered her dressing room, and slammed the door. Minutes later, a light tapping sounded at the door.

"Five minutes until curtain," Private Mosier called out before proceeding down the hallway.

Teddi's palms moistened and her heart began to pound in her chest. She gave herself one final glance in the mirror and opened the door. Phillip was moving toward the opposite side of the stage for his entry. She gave him a faint smile, but if he returned the greeting, it was hidden in the shadows of the darkened stage. She shouldn't have been so brusque. After all, he was probably a bundle of nerves, trying to remember his lines as well as stage directions and costume changes. An apology was in order and she'd see to it—unless he caused her no end of embarrassment during the performance!

The orchestra was positioned in front of the large stage and was just completing the overture when the director gazed about, apparently assuring himself that the actors were properly aligned to step onto the stage at his prompting. On the other side of the curtain, the chattering of small children mingled with the murmuring of adults in the nearly full auditorium. An occasional cough could be heard; then, finally, all was silent except for the whirring of the curtain as it rose toward the ceiling.

Up, up the giant mural began to roll until, without warning, the whirring sound momentarily ceased, causing one side of the curtain to hoist higher than the other. Suddenly, the painted scene of the Bay of Naples and Mt. Vesuvius began to roll up askew. Muffled laughter finally gave way to joyful merriment before General Yorke finally called out from the audience, "Steady there! Dress to the left, men!" With renewed vigor, the curtain began to rise, this time lifting the painted drapery to the ceiling in proper fashion.

The director waited until the crowd had settled, and then the actors began their first scene in earnest. However, Teddi's attempts to remain calm were falling short of perfection. She was rushing through her opening lines, and her voice was warbling so violently that the words she was speaking were barely distinguishable. The director's wild motioning for her to slow down seemed only to make her speak more rapidly. She couldn't seem to gain control of herself and gave momentary consideration to rushing offstage. Instead, she turned on cue, watched, and listened as Phillip made his entrance and recited his lines in a calm, self-assured voice.

With a practiced ease, he moved to where Teddi stood, took her hand in his, and whispered into her ear, "Relax, Teddi. The audience has come to have fun—there's no need to be nervous." He squeezed her hand and gave her a wink as he moved to his proper mark on the stage. Taking a deep breath, she forced herself to calmly recite her next lines. With each word, the recitation of her part and moving about the stage became more comfortable. By the second act, she felt certain that she was having every bit as much fun as Phillip.

When the final farewell scene arrived, Phillip swept her into his arms, captured her lips with his own, and kissed her soundly. It took her breath away, and she hadn't fully recovered by the time the curtain began its ascent for their bows. A roar of applause thundered through the auditorium as the actors joined hands, stepped forward, and all of them bent in unison for a final ovation.

"What were you thinking?" she asked as they continued bowing.

"I can't hear you," Phillip replied while pointing toward his ear.

"I said, what were you thinking?" she shrieked into his ear.

"I was thinking about making the play as realistic as possible. It would have been obvious to the audience if I had only pretended to kiss you," he said while giving her a broad smile.

"It's not the way we rehearsed it," she retorted.

"Well, of course not. Gardner's a married man. It wouldn't be seemly for you to be kissing a married man. I, on the other hand, am not married, not even betrothed, so it seemed the proper thing to do. You know, in the interest of giving the audience our very best performance. It was, after all, merely a performance," he hastily added.

"Well, of course I realize that," she replied a little too quickly.

"Then why are you making such a fuss?" he inquired, moving back as the curtain made its final descent.

She remained silent, knowing she dare not speak the truth.

He would surely be appalled to hear that his kiss had sent ripples of excitement coursing through her body, that she had enjoyed the excitement of his lips against her own, and that she was still taking pleasure in the warmth of his kiss that lingered on her lips. Or would he be so horrified? The kiss had seemed genuine; yet, when questioned, he had been swift to say that he was merely acting his part. Why was she even entertaining such silly thoughts? A man was interested in having only a pretty woman on his arm, one that caused heads to turn, and she, with her plain face and imperfect figure, could never be such a woman.

seven

"Are you by yourself?" Teddi questioned, attempting to peer around Jonathan as he entered her dressing room.

"Mother and Father said they would join us at the party, and George found several young ladies to keep him busy," Jonathan answered. "Were you expecting anyone else?"

"No, I don't suppose I was. Thank you for waiting, Jonathan."

"It's an honor to escort the star of the play," he joked. "You were very good, do you know that?"

"I was frightened senseless, until. . ."

"Until Phillip came on stage. You were rushing your lines a bit before then, but he seemed to have a calming effect upon you. He does that to me, too. Good man, don't you think?"

"I don't know him well enough to know if he's a good man or not. We'd better get going," Teddi replied, fastening her woolen cape.

"Don't know him well enough? You were in love with him when you were ten," Jonathan retorted.

"Thirteen!" Teddi quickly corrected.

"Okay, thirteen, but you *do* remember."

"Remember what? That my big brother's friend rebuffed me? Of course I remember. It's a painful memory."

"Even after all these years?"

"You wouldn't understand; men think differently than women. You'll come closer to understanding the concept once you finally decide to settle down and have a serious relationship," Teddi retorted.

"But *that* wasn't a serious relationship, Teddi. You were thirteen, just a kid. And it was, after all, one-sided. Phillip didn't even know about your feelings until—"

"I made a fool of myself?"

"I didn't say that, Teddi. You didn't make a fool of yourself. You were a young girl infatuated with your big brother's best friend. You told him that you cared for him. That's not making a fool of yourself," Jonathan countered.

"I don't want to discuss this any longer. Besides, I'm already late for the cast party," she replied, gently pushing him aside and moving out the door.

"Teddi, Mother told me about Herbert Albright. I'm truly sorry, but if he was so shallow as to be drawn away by the first pretty woman that passed his way, you're better off without him. But you shouldn't use his unchivalrous behavior as a measurement of all men. Phillip and Herbert are two entirely different people," Jonathan argued as he rushed to catch up with her.

"Oh, for goodness' sake, Jonathan, will you please quit defending Phillip? Let's just go to the party," she insisted.

The enlisted men's dining hall was ablaze with light. A mixture of laughter and chatter filled the night air as Jonathan pulled open the door for his sister. A sea of men in dark blue dress uniforms and women in brightly colored gowns parted as they made their way through the room.

"May I have the first dance?" General Yorke inquired, handing Teddi's cape and bonnet to her brother. "Jonathan will see to your wraps."

Teddi giggled as she watched her brother feign indignation. "I thought that surely I would have the privilege of the first dance. After all, I escorted her, Father," Jonathan argued.

"Perhaps, but age does have its advantages, my boy. Now, do as you're told," he said, genially dismissing his son with a wave of his arm. "Come, my dear. I'll show these young fellows how it's supposed to be done," he said, leading her onto the gleaming hardwood floor.

In keeping with the season, the large room was festooned with green cedar branches adorned with red berries and tied with wide red-and-white ribbons. The dining tables had been moved along the walls and were now draped with crisp white tablecloths and laden with holiday delicacies of every variety. Centerpieces crafted from dried flowers and greenery were flanked on either side by tall, flickering candles; the festive combination graced each of the serving tables. Isabelle's cherished sterling punch bowl was centered on a table at the rear of the room, its highly polished silver reflecting a rainbow's array of colors as the dancers whirled by.

"Wonderful performance, my dear. Watching you up on that stage made me very proud. It was like old times, seeing you and Phillip having fun together," Clayton commented.

"Old times? I don't remember ever having much fun with Phillip. But I do remember chasing after him and Jonathan, begging them to let me join in their fun," Teddi replied. First her brother, and now her father. Why did everyone have to keep bringing Phillip into the conversation?

"Ah, but isn't that the way of all children? Half of their time spent playing is making it look as though they're having so much fun that others want to join in?" Clayton asked.

"Perhaps. But if you're the one chasing after them and begging to be a part of their games, it isn't such fun. Besides, that was years ago. Phillip and I are both adults now, and the drama we performed tonight wasn't a child's game."

"Well, it certainly appeared that Phillip was having a grand time—especially that last scene. But now that I think about it, he looked as though he was taking that kiss pretty seriously," Clayton replied, giving her a boisterous chuckle just as the music ceased.

"You're letting your imagination and propensity toward matchmaking get the best of you, Father. It was nothing but acting," Teddi replied defensively.

"I'm not so sure," he argued. "I'd better get you back to your brother, or he'll be complaining that I've stolen you away for the whole evening," Clayton continued as he began to direct Teddi toward her brother.

Helen Hanson was clinging to Phillip's arm, obviously mesmerized by his charms as the two of them stood chatting with Jonathan. Teddi attempted to guide her father in another direction, but his bulk proved more difficult to maneuver than she had anticipated, causing them to end up directly in the midst of the threesome that she had hoped to avoid.

"Well, here she is, fit as a fiddle and ready to dance the night away," the general announced as he deposited Teddi between her brother and Phillip and walked off toward his wife.

"Oh, Teddi, I was just telling Phillip what a simply divine performance the two of you gave us this evening. If I had known that *Phillip* was going to play the lead, I would have auditioned for the part," Helen purred.

"Perhaps next time, Helen. You do seem to have a flair for the dramatic," Teddi responded as she watched Helen tighten her hold on Phillip's arm.

The band director lifted his arms to signal the next dance, and Jonathan quickly reached out and grasped Helen's free hand. "Come along, Helen. Let's permit the stars of the show to have this dance," he said, deftly moving her onto the dance floor before she could protest.

"Shall we?" Phillip asked, holding out his hand toward Teddi.

She nodded her agreement, and soon they were circling the floor, his hand resting lightly at her waist. Her palms were damp. She could feel Phillip's eyes upon her, and she longed for some sensible thought to enter her mind, some coy or amusing anecdote that might serve to fill the silence between them.

"You have quite a talent on the stage, Teddi. I was wondering if I could convince you to direct the children in the church pageant this year?"

"I believe Colonel Lane asked Mrs. Bennett to perform that duty several months ago—before his retirement," Teddi replied. "But should she decide she needs assistance, I'll be more than pleased to help. However, Mrs. Bennett is accustomed to working with the children, so you need not worry. She'll do an excellent job."

"I see. And who's in charge of the oyster supper? I hear that's one of the major events of the holiday season," Phillip inquired.

"My mother, although I wish that she hadn't agreed to do it again this year. It becomes a family event, with plenty of work for all of us. Of course with Jonathan and George here, it may not be as difficult this year. I'll suggest she keep them busy."

"So both of your brothers will be here for Christmas?"

"They'll leave after New Year's Day. It's going to be great fun having them here to enjoy the holidays. I know my parents are delighted that Jonathan and George could both manage to remain throughout the holidays."

Phillip nodded. "That is good news."

"Aren't you going home for the holidays? To see your parents, I mean," Teddi quickly added.

"No. I don't think the army would consider a request for leave so soon after my arrival. Besides, being with your family is almost the same as being with mine," Phillip remarked, giving her a broad smile. "Would you like some punch?" he offered as the music ended and they left the dance floor.

"That would be nice," Teddi agreed, watching as he strode toward the rear of the hall.

"Put in a good word for me, would you?" Helen whispered, grasping Teddi by the arm and pulling her close.

"With my brother?" Teddi asked, now giving Helen her full attention.

"No, silly, with Phillip. Tell him that I'd make a perfect military wife. Isn't he just the most handsome man in the room?" she asked as Phillip walked toward them with two silver punch cups filled to the brim.

"Why, thank you," Helen cooed as she extended her hand toward one of the cups. "How very thoughtful of you, Phillip."

Phillip handed the other cup to Teddi, glancing first at Teddi before allowing his sight to rest upon Helen.

"This *was* for me, wasn't it?" Helen asked, in her most charming voice.

"If you are in need of a cool drink, it is most certainly for you. I'm pleased that I could be of assistance," Phillip gallantly added.

"Well, dear me, when you came in my direction, I just naturally assumed you were bringing the punch for me, rather for us—for you and me to share," she continued explaining as she determinedly moved closer to his side.

"Actually, I had gotten the punch for Teddi and me. I assumed you were busy on the dance floor. But, as I said, I don't mind coming to your aid," he answered.

"Let me thank you properly by permitting you the privilege of the next dance," Helen crooned. "I'm sure that one of Teddi's brothers will be more than happy to escort her onto the dance floor."

"I would love to, Helen, but I've already signed Teddi's dance card for the next dance and Mrs. Yorke's for the one following Teddi's. But if you're free after that, I'll be back," Phillip replied.

"I'll be waiting right here," Helen cooed as Phillip and Teddi returned to the dance floor.

The band seemed to play on indeterminately and Helen paced along the edge of the floor until Phillip finally returned Teddi to the punch table.

"What did you say to him?" Helen whispered as she

sidled up to Teddi.

"About what?" Teddi absentmindedly inquired as she watched Phillip and her mother take to the dance floor.

"Me, of course," Helen tersely replied as she tucked a ringlet of dark hair back into place. Her large, bow-shaped lips were formed into a pout that reminded Teddi of a two year old.

"Your name didn't come up," Teddi replied.

"*You* were supposed to bring it up, remember? I specifically asked you to put in a good word for me. I should have realized that you were eyeing him for yourself, now that Herbert's walked out on you," Helen rebutted, her razor-sharp words meeting their mark.

Teddi shrunk back from the attack, her eyes darting about the room in hope of finding some point of refuge. *Jonathan!* He was making his way across the dance floor toward where she stood. Without a word, she shoved her punch cup into Helen's free hand and walked onto the floor, meeting Jonathan midway.

"I presume you'd like to dance?" Jonathan said with a laugh.

"We don't have to dance. Just get me away from Helen Hanson and her vicious tongue," Teddi answered.

"What's Helen's problem? Not enough beaux, or no special beau?"

"She wanted me to tell Phillip what a catch she'd make for him. When I didn't take the first opportunity available to pass along the information, she became insulting."

"You should have just told her that when the right moment presented itself, you'd talk to him," Jonathan instructed.

"Why should I be Helen Hanson's matchmaker? She's never had the time of day for me unless she wanted some favor. Furthermore, I don't think that I'd be doing Phillip any favor by telling him that Helen is considering him as her next beau," Teddi told him.

"Hmmm. You wouldn't be jealous that other women find Phillip desirable, would you?"

"Of course not. Why should I be? He's nothing to me."

"You sound a bit defensive, dear sister. Sure you're not still carrying a torch for our old family friend after all these years?"

"I'm not carrying a torch for anyone. If Helen had asked me to act as a go-between with you or George, I wouldn't have done that, either. My refusal to help has nothing to do with Phillip. It's Helen. I'd have to see some dramatic changes in her behavior before I'd ever speak on her behalf," Teddi explained.

"I see," Jonathan replied, nodding his head.

"You don't believe me, do you?"

"It doesn't matter what I think, Teddi. You know what's in your heart. I do know that Phillip is a good man and would make a fine husband and father. And I think he's reached a point in his life at which he's ready to settle down—with the right woman, of course. Not with someone as shallow and devious as Helen Hanson. Perhaps you can think of someone who might qualify?" Jonathan asked, his voice filled with seriousness.

"Tell me, Jonathan, is that truly your assessment or Phillip's? Because from my point of view, he seems much more interested in attracting beauty than avoiding shallow or devious behavior," Teddi replied.

"Well, I'm sure that he wouldn't hold beauty against a woman," Jonathan said, giving her a laugh. "Ouch!"

"Oh, I'm so sorry. Did I hurt your foot, big brother?" she asked as they continued to move around the dance floor.

"You intentionally stepped on my foot, Teddi," Jonathan accused.

"You're right—I did," she admitted with a sweet smile curving her lips. "And you're intentionally trying to get me to admit I have feelings for Phillip. But I don't. At least not the kind you're talking about."

"Well, what kind *do* you have, then?" he doggedly insisted.

"The bad kind. As I told you earlier, Phillip treated me shabbily when I was a little girl, and I haven't forgotten that."

"What did you expect? That he would write long love letters pledging his undying devotion to my pudgy little sister? Come on, Teddi."

"He could have at least acknowledged the letters. Even a short note telling me I was a nice little girl, but I was too young for him would have sufficed. Something—anything. He could have returned my gift. I certainly suffered Father's wrath for giving away my sleigh bell," Teddi answered, her voice filled with remorse.

"Sleigh bell?" Jonathan stopped dancing in the middle of the floor. The other couples were swirling about them as he stood there looking dumbstruck. "He *did* return your sleigh bell, Teddi. He gave your charm back to me years ago. You remember that little, carved wooden box of mine? I put your sleigh bell in there for safekeeping, and the charm has remained there ever since. I'm telling you the truth, I promise. I'll send it to you as soon as I return to Washington," Jonathan continued.

They were standing in the middle of the dance floor. The music had ceased playing, and the floor had emptied. Now the other couples stood watching the brother and sister who were so engrossed in their own conversation that they seemed unaware of their surroundings.

"Jonathan Yorke, how *could* you?" Teddi responded.

"I told you—I forgot. Don't make it sound like I intentionally set out to hurt you," Jonathan replied.

"Do you remember the punishment I suffered because I gave away that charm?"

"You spent most of the summer indoors helping Mother, as

I recall," he said with a sheepish grin.

"Not *that* punishment. Don't you remember that Father had always given me a charm every year on my birthday? When I gave away the sleigh bell, he told me there would be no more charms. He said that if I didn't value his gift enough to keep it, he wouldn't purchase any more charms for my bracelet. And I've never received another since then," Teddi said in an anguish-filled voice. "And to think you've had my sleigh bell hidden away. . . ."

"It wasn't hidden, Teddi. I put it away for safekeeping. You make it sound as though I was purposely trying to hurt you."

"Perhaps it wasn't intentional, Jonathan, but that didn't change the outcome, did it?"

"No, and I'm not shirking my responsibility. But, if you're going to direct your wrath at me, I hope you'll let Phillip know that I've set the record straight," Jonathan replied. "And I'll explain to Father," he quickly added.

"Are you two going to spend the remainder of the evening entertaining us?" General Yorke called out from where he stood by one of the serving tables. "The rest of us are going to eat some of this sumptuous-looking food."

Teddi looked at her father, feeling as though she'd been pulled from a trance, and then glanced about the room. Everyone was staring at them, and she could feel the heat rising to her cheeks. Jonathan, on the other hand, seemed to be enjoying the unsolicited attention, as he gazed about and gave the crowd a winsome smile.

"Oh, Jonathan, quit making a further spectacle of yourself," Teddi chided as she pulled her brother off the dance floor. The *last* thing she wanted was more embarrassment and another story for the local gossips.

"Come along, my dear. You and Phillip are supposed to begin the serving line," Isabelle instructed her daughter.

"You and Jonathan certainly appeared to be engrossed in

your conversation," Phillip commented after they had filled their plates.

"Part of that conversation was about you."

"Really?" he asked, his gaze immediately drawn to her eyes.

"Do you remember the silver sleigh bell charm that I gave you years ago? When you were moving away to Fort MacKinac?"

Phillip nodded his head. "I remember."

"Jonathan just now told me that you returned my charm years ago. Unfortunately, he failed to give it back to me. So I owe you an apology. All these years I thought you'd probably discarded it or, worse yet, given it to someone else," she said, looking down at her plate as she murmured the last few words.

"My dear Teddi, I would never have given your silver charm to another girl. Besides, I had already returned it to your brother before I started buying gifts for girls," he said with a chuckle. "Does this mean that perhaps you've forgiven me, and we can be friends?"

"Yes, Phillip, you're forgiven, and I apologize for behaving so boorishly since your arrival," Teddi replied.

"Your apology is accepted. Why don't we seal our new friendship by doing something special together? What about the skating party tomorrow—may I be your escort?"

She thought for only a moment. "Yes, Phillip, I'd love to go to the skating party with you. Provided you don't mind Jonathan and George tagging along. They're not about to stay home when there's a party to be enjoyed."

"The more the merrier. It will be a good time, I'm sure of it," he said. "You can't imagine how relieved I am that we've finally settled our differences," he said, giving her a broad smile.

eight

The morning dawned crisp, the pale blue sky laden with heavy white clouds. Teddi's father referred to them as "snow clouds," more out of his desire for snow than any weather-predicting ability, she suspected. The bedroom window was frosted both inside and out, evidence of a significant drop in the temperature during the night. Teddi burrowed a little more deeply under the covers. The embers in the bedroom fireplace had grown cold hours ago, and the only thing that would now warm the chilled bedroom was heat rising from the kitchen below. She could hear Florence downstairs. It wouldn't be long until a fire was blazing in the kitchen and breakfast was cooking. Teddi decided she would venture out from the warmth of her nest once the smell of frying bacon wafted up the stairway and drifted into her room.

She rolled over and relished the idea of the day that lay ahead. After breakfast she would need to check several patients at the hospital and study her Sunday school lesson; after lunch, she'd go off to the skating party. Phillip hadn't mentioned if he'd be at the hospital this morning, but surely he would be there to see to his patients' progress. The thought of seeing Phillip almost made her want to get out of bed. Almost, but not quite, she decided.

"Teddi! We're going to start breakfast without you if you don't come downstairs this minute," General Yorke called.

"Coming, Father," she replied as she quickly set about buttoning her white percale shirtwaist.

Teddi was fashioning a bow of dark red silk under the collar when she finally entered the dining room several minutes later.

"Were you planning on having Florence fix you a separate breakfast today?" her father asked as Teddi settled into one of the straight-backed dining-room chairs and then waited for Jonathan to pass the tureen of scrambled eggs.

"No, I would never expect special favors from Florence—unlike some other people seated at this table. If I'm late for a meal, I'm perfectly capable of heating up leftovers or finding something to fix for myself—also unlike some others seated at this table," Teddi replied with a note of satisfaction in her voice. "Isn't that right, Florence?" she asked as the maid carried a pot of fresh coffee into the room.

"Yes, indeed. I don't think I've ever been asked to perform any extra duties for you, Miss Yorke, except maybe to press a special shirtwaist, or soak and wash bandages for the hospital patients, or air out your bedding and pillows every day, or. . ."

"Guess she got you on that one, Teddi," the general chortled.

"You do enjoy getting the best of a situation, Father. But I'm not going to let it ruin my good spirits."

"Are you in good spirits because you're off to work at the hospital while George and I relax here at home?" Jonathan gibed.

"No, I'm in good spirits because there's an ice-skating party this afternoon, and Phillip offered to escort me."

"Is that a fact? Nobody mentioned the skating party to me," George sulked. "Surely you planned on inviting Jonathan and me along."

"As if I could stop the two of you from going to a party, invited or not," Teddi replied, giving her brother a smile. "I told Phillip that I was sure the two of you would be tagging along."

"Ah, we'd best get some extra rest this morning so we'll be well rested for a busy afternoon of skating with the gorgeous young ladies from Junction City. They *will* be attending, won't they?" Jonathan inquired.

"I'm sure the young ladies *and* the young men from Junction City will be in attendance," Teddi teased as she rose from the table. "Well, I'm off to the hospital. I should be back by eleven o'clock."

"Wait, Teddi. I'll take you in the sleigh," Jonathan offered.

"That's not necessary. I go to the hospital by myself every day. Besides, you'll just have to come back later, and you may be busy helping Mother with her chores by then!"

"But I *want* to take you," he insisted.

They had hardly gotten into the sleigh when Teddi realized just why Jonathan was so determined to accompany her. He questioned her incessantly, desiring every detail of what had occurred between Phillip and her. He wanted to know why she had suddenly accepted an invitation to attend a social function with Phillip, if he had explained the mishap regarding the missing charm, and if she had been gracious in her acceptance of his explanation. Jonathan absolutely insisted upon knowing if she had apologized for her rude behavior. By the time they arrived at the hospital, Teddi had fielded more questions than would a soldier being interrogated at his own court-martial.

"For the first time, Jonathan, I must say that I'm glad to get away from you," Teddi said with a sigh of relief as he offered his hand to assist her out of the sleigh.

"Too many questions for you?" he asked with a laugh.

"Far too many, and no means of escape. I'm going to remember this device the next time I want to wheedle information from you or George," she promised.

"It won't be necessary. We have no secrets," he answered, taking the reins into his gloved hands. "I'll be back at eleven, and I'll spend the next several hours making up a list of additional questions I forgot to ask."

She started to respond, but he laughed, slapped the reins, and waved over his shoulder as the horses jerked the sleigh into motion. Teddi stood listening as the jingling of the sleigh bells grew faint in the distance.

"Good morning," Phillip greeted Teddi as she walked into the hospital. "It's a good day for ice-skating, don't you think?"

"Good morning to you. And, yes, it's a perfect day for ice-skating. By the way, at breakfast this morning I mentioned that there was an ice-skating party this afternoon. Jonathan and George didn't surprise me. They immediately sought an invitation," she told Phillip while hanging her cloak on a wooden hook in the vestibule.

"Did you tell them I didn't need any more competition for the pretty, young women?" he asked, giving her a laugh. "They are more than welcome, and I'm sure you told them so," he added.

"Yes, but knowing my brothers, I imagine they would come along anyway, welcome or not. I'd better get busy. Jonathan said he would come back for me at eleven. I want to finish my Bible study before going skating this afternoon," she told him.

"Well, that's certainly a praiseworthy endeavor. Fortunately, my sermon has been prepared for several days, or I would need to give up the party this afternoon. I'll be in my office if you need me. There are some medical records I want to review. Just in case I don't see you again before you leave the hospital, I'll plan to come by your quarters at two o'clock."

"That will be fine," she replied as she exited the room and walked down the hallway.

Teddi quickly made her way through the ward, checking each patient, making notations on the charts that hung on their beds, and moving on to the next patient. She attempted to make small talk with the men, but her mind kept wandering back to Phillip's remark about her brothers providing him with competition for the pretty, young ladies. Since he was escorting her to the skating party, why was he concerned about the other girls who would be attending? After all, if he wanted to keep company with one of the other girls, why hadn't he invited one of them? Or had he merely been jesting—making a casual remark that meant nothing at all. Most likely she was spending the morning worrying about something that was of absolutely no consequence. What was that verse in the Bible? *"Take therefore no thought for the morrow: for the morrow shall take thought for the things of itself. Sufficient unto the day is the evil thereof."* Yes, that was it—she was borrowing trouble. Trouble that would only spoil the good time that she intended to have later today!

❧

Phillip leaned back in the leather-upholstered chair that sat behind his desk and, with a deliberate snap, closed the medical book he had been reading for the past hour. If he hurried, he would have time to get back to his quarters, change out of his uniform, and arrive at the Yorkes' on time. Good sense dictated that he should have gone directly to his quarters after having lunch in the dining hall, but during the noon meal he had decided there was sufficient time to catch up on some long overdue reading. Now, he wished he'd taken the book instead. Muttering to himself, he locked the office door and strode out of the hospital, anxious to be on his way.

An afternoon of skating would provide additional opportunity for him to socialize with some of the young adults from Junction City. And perhaps he would be fortunate enough to spark some interest in the Bible study and social activities he hoped the parishioners of the chapel would sponsor throughout the winter. Fortunately, he was now back in Teddi's good graces. She could provide valuable information about the folks living in and around the military reservation and might even agree to make arrangements for some of the activities.

His mind was filled with ideas as he bounded up the steps to the Yorkes' quarters a short time later, knocked on the front door, and was met by George, who was already wearing his coat and heavy gloves.

"Teddi and Jonathan were sure you had stood us up, but I assured them you wouldn't do such a thing," George said as he held open the door.

"Don't believe a thing he tells you. I thought you might have an ill patient at the hospital," Teddi quickly defended. "It was Jonathan who commented that you'd probably found better company!"

"How could I possibly find better company?" he asked with a broad smile. "Let me help you with your coat," he offered, his hand brushing against hers as he took the coat.

"We're leaving, Mother," Jonathan called out as he bounded out of the kitchen with several of Florence's freshly baked sugar cookies in his hand, his coat flapping about as he made his way out the door and down the front steps.

"I think you may want to fasten your coat and make sure you have some gloves," Teddi instructed as Jonathan piled into the sleigh.

They all laughed as he stuffed the remaining cookie in his mouth and retrieved a pair of gloves from deep inside his coat pockets, waving them in the air.

"I have gloves," he announced when he'd finally swallowed the mouthful of cookies.

"Good! Then we're on our way," Phillip announced, flicking the reins. The horses snorted and shook their heads, as if to ward off the icy chill, before beginning their journey.

The runners of the sleigh cut through the ice-crusted layer of snow, which broke the serenity that blanketed the vast expanse of rolling hills and prairie. The group's laughter echoed through the quiet countryside as a light snow began to fall. However, the flurries only added to the excitement of the day and somehow seemed appropriate for the first skating party of the season.

"You know what's wrong with this sleigh?" Teddi asked as they were nearing the creek.

"Nothing!" the three men called out and then laughed cheerfully at their unified response.

"Yes, there *is* something wrong with it," Teddi insisted.

"Please tell me, and I'll see that it's remedied," Phillip replied with a glint in his eye.

"This sleigh doesn't have any bells. It *needs* sleigh bells!"

"Well, of course. We all know that sleigh bells are a necessity. Otherwise, a sleigh just won't operate properly, Phillip. How could you possibly own a sleigh without bells?" Jonathan bantered.

"Teddi has a valid point. I rather like the sound of sleigh bells myself," Phillip agreed. "I'll have to see if I can rectify the problem. Thank you for bringing it to my attention," he added.

"I'm sure that Teddi would be happy to help you find just the right sleigh bells," George offered.

"Oh, stop it, George, or I'll tell all the girls that you're not worth their time," Teddi retorted.

"Looks like quite a crowd has already gathered," Jonathan said as they approached the creek. "Give me your hand, Teddi. I'll help you out of the sleigh."

A small group of men and women were already on the ice as the foursome walked down to the edge of the creek. Several skaters were warming themselves at a crackling fire that was being fueled with branches from a nearby dead tree. The women, with brightly colored knitted scarves tied tightly around their heads, were discussing whether to move away from the fire while the men were devising a plan to pull a sled onto the ice with a heavy piece of rope.

"Let's go over to the fire, and you can make some introductions," Phillip suggested while her brothers quickly nodded their heads in agreement.

"Good idea, Phillip," Jonathan chimed in. "I'm hoping I

can find an agreeable young lady I can escort to all the Christmas parties I've been hearing about."

"Only one? I would think you'd want to find several. That way you'd have a bit of variety," Phillip said with a chuckle.

"Is that what *you* prefer—variety?" Teddi inquired.

There was an edge to her voice that took Phillip by surprise.

"Well, I wouldn't put it quite that way. I'm looking for a woman who has the same beliefs and values. Someone who loves the Lord. . ."

"And the army," George chimed in, laughing at his own remark.

"That too," Phillip agreed.

"Sounds like you've just described our Teddi," Jonathan remarked while giving his sister an exaggerated wink.

Jonathan's statement caught Phillip off guard and was obviously embarrassing to Teddi. The chilly December weather had caused Teddi's cheeks to turn pink, but her brother's casual remark had now intensified the color to flaming red.

"Of course, a woman of beauty is always agreeable," George observed.

"Not necessarily," Phillip countered. "Sometimes beautiful women rely solely on their physical attributes to get them through life. I've met some lovely women who were shallow."

"Well, I would love to continue this discussion, but I feel it's my duty to escort one of these young ladies onto the ice," Jonathan bantered. "That is, if you're ever going to make those promised introductions, dear sister."

Teddi poked him in the side and began to lead him toward a young woman not far from the group, with Phillip and George following along behind.

"No, *that* one," Jonathan instructed, pointing toward a girl with unruly golden locks peeking out from beneath a cream-colored, woolen scarf.

Teddi smiled. "You don't agree with Phillip, I take it. You want beauty rather than—"

"Some women have both," Jonathan asserted.

"I really think you'd find Ruth Ann much more to your liking," Teddi argued.

"No, I want to meet *her*," Jonathan insisted while pulling Teddi in the young woman's direction.

"Fine, but I don't think. . ."

"Just introduce me," Jonathan insisted. "You can introduce George to Ruth Ann, can't she, George?"

George merely nodded his head as Phillip watched the scene in amusement. It was obvious that things weren't going as Teddi had planned, and he was finding her mounting frustration with Jonathan entertaining.

"Good afternoon, Margaret. I would like to introduce you to my brother, Jonathan Yorke. Jonathan is visiting us at Fort Riley for the holidays. Jonathan, this is Margaret Willoughby," Teddi said in her most formal voice.

The girl looked back and forth between Teddi and Jonathan and appeared somewhat confused, but finally gave Jonathan a tentative smile. "Nice to meet you. Would you mind helping me with my skates?" Margaret asked, dangling the pair of skates from her gloved hand.

"I'd be delighted. Why don't you sit on that stump over there, and I'll get them clamped," Jonathan suggested as the twosome walked away.

"Are *you* interested in meeting Ruth Ann?" Teddi asked, turning to stare at George.

George compliantly nodded his head in agreement, while Phillip laughed aloud. "What are you laughing at?" Teddi asked, obviously irritated with both of the men.

"I think George knows better than to say he doesn't want to meet Ruth Ann. If he values his life, that is," Phillip replied, still laughing.

"All three of you are beginning to wear on my patience," Teddi responded as she marched off toward where Ruth Ann was standing.

Phillip walked alongside George, both of them following closely behind Teddi as she approached the dark-haired, young woman and quickly made introductions. George and Ruth Ann were soon making their way toward the ice when Teddi turned toward Phillip.

"And which of the young women do *you* wish to meet?" Teddi asked.

"I've already met her. Would *you* skate with me?" he asked, extending his hand.

"Well, yes, I'd love to," Teddi replied, obviously pleased by the invitation.

They joined several other couples on the ice, gliding down the creek's frozen path and then back toward the widest part where most of the skating crowd was congregated. The skaters were moving gracefully on the ice, a canopy of frozen branches extending overhead as a light snow continued to fall. Suddenly, waving arms and a woman's voice calling from the creek's edge broke the beautiful winter scene.

"Phillip! Over here!" A woman's shrill voice screamed from the distance, her arms raised high above her head and a red scarf swinging from her hand as she waved her arms back and forth.

"Is that. . .?"

"Helen? Absolutely," Teddi replied.

"Perhaps we should go over. If she keeps screaming like that, she's liable to cause a crack in the ice," Phillip joked.

"I don't think she's quite *that* loud, but she probably won't stop until you go over there," Teddi agreed.

He really didn't want to leave the ice. He and Teddi were having a wonderful conversation, discussing everything from operating procedures to Scripture interpretation, and Phillip had been thoroughly enjoying himself. Teddi seemed to have an opinion about everything, yet she was willing to listen to his viewpoint and even change her beliefs if given valid reasons for doing so. She was indeed refreshing—a woman with spirit and substance, he decided, just as they approached the lovely Helen Hanson.

nine

Teddi stood by the bonfire, forcing herself to concentrate on the conversation taking place around her. She couldn't do it. Her gaze continued to follow the handsome-appearing couple skating arm in arm, now gliding down the creek and slowly leaving her field of vision. Moving around the edge of the fire, she repositioned herself and hoped to gain a better view, but they were now out of sight.

"Helen certainly has her cap set for the new doctor, doesn't she?" Mattie Fielding stated while shaking her head.

"He's a preacher, too, not just a doctor," Teddi countered.

"Doctor, preacher, lawyer, store clerk—makes no difference. There's no stopping that girl once she sets her sights on someone."

"Did she tell you that she's interested in Captain Hamilton?"

"Yes, but she wouldn't have to *tell* me. Just watching her is evidence enough," Mattie replied with a giggle.

"But what did she say?"

"That he was the best-looking single man to be stationed at Fort Riley in ages and that she planned to make him her very own. She did mention that she thought your brother Jonathan might interest her even more, but he'd soon be leaving. So she decided not to waste valuable time with Jonathan. I think she was fearful that someone else might snag Captain Hamilton if she decided to spend time with your brother."

"I see," was all Teddi could manage, suddenly thankful to see George and Ruth Ann approaching.

"We've decided to leave. Ruth Ann needs to be home soon, and I've agreed to escort her," George informed his sister.

"How?" Teddi inquired. "You don't have a sleigh."

"She came with several other couples. The men said they would take me back to the post once we've escorted the girls home," he replied, obviously anxious to be on his way.

Teddi stared after her brother, wishing that he and Ruth Ann had remained to keep her company. But at least they seemed to enjoy being with each other, and *that* was satisfying, she decided as she watched the sleigh move off toward town.

The silence after their departure was soon broken by Mattie's shrill voice cutting through the crisp air. "He is rather handsome, don't you agree?" she asked, looking out across the ice just as Helen and Phillip made their reappearance.

"What? Oh, yes, extremely handsome. She'd be a fool to let my brother slip away," Teddi responded.

"Not your brother, Captain Hamilton," Mattie corrected, giving Teddi an exasperated look. "I told Helen there was nobody who could turn the captain's head if *she* took an interest in him. There's no one who can hold a candle to Helen, except Margaret Willoughby. And who's going to be interested in Margaret? Except your brother," she added, noting Jonathan coming toward them with Margaret in tow.

"So you think it's only beauty that matters to men?" Teddi asked.

"Well, of course, silly. They all make those perfunctory statements about wanting a woman who's a good cook, can keep a spotless house, is devout in her Christian beliefs, and is intelligent, but when it comes down to actually choosing a wife, they pick the most comely one that will have them. You, of all people, should know that!" Mattie added.

The words stung like salt in an open wound, causing Teddi to flinch. Yes, she knew what people thought. After all, she believed the same thing. When given the choice of a beautiful, young woman, Herbert Albright had succumbed, leaving plain, thick-waisted, intelligent Teddi at the altar. Well, not really at the altar, she told herself. She and Herbert had set their wedding date for May 23, but he had betrayed her many months before the arranged day. Besides, she reasoned, it was better to suffer the humiliation now as his former fiancée than as his wife. But Mattie's comments served as a reminder that gossip was not soon forgotten, nor people soon forgiven. Why, even Margaret Willoughby's name had come up in Mattie's comments, and how long had it been since *that* consequential day?

The thought caught her by surprise. She was just as guilty as Mattie. Perhaps she hadn't put words to her thoughts, but she had certainly discouraged her brother from meeting Margaret. Hadn't Margaret come before the body of believers confessing her sin, repenting, and seeking forgiveness a long time ago?

The congregation had listened; the preacher had told Margaret that she had been correct in coming forward to confess her sin. He had gone a step further and assured her that not only had God forgiven her, but the body of believers had done the same. Unfortunately, it hadn't been altogether true. Oh, people had spoken to her when it was absolutely necessary, and she was usually included in activities for which a general invitation was extended. But nobody had befriended her; nobody had *truly* accepted her; nobody had ever extended a special invitation to Margaret Willoughby. Not after hearing that Sunday morning confession a year ago.

Teddi's shoulders slumped, and her head dropped as she acknowledged her own participation in such disappointing behavior. Certainly her actions didn't exemplify Christ's teachings. Who was she to treat another human being with such contempt? Especially one who had been so brave, one who had followed the Bible's teachings, one who had done what was required of God to assure forgiveness. The shame of Teddi's behavior welled up inside her until she thought it would cut off her breath and choke her.

"You seem deep in thought," Jonathan remarked as he moved alongside Teddi.

She startled at his voice, glanced around, and was eye to eye with Margaret. "I told Jonathan not to disturb you. I thought you appeared to be praying," Margaret said, her voice barely a whisper.

It was obvious Margaret was unsure how she would be received. There was a tentativeness about her, a wounded look that Teddi had never before noticed.

"You're right, Margaret. I was praying. Asking for God's forgiveness. And now I need to ask for yours," Teddi replied. "I've treated you unkindly, not shown you the friendship you deserve. I've shunned you when what you did was courageous and true to God's Word. I'm afraid I've been guilty of not truly forgiving you of your past mistakes and, worse yet, being judgmental. I don't know what I would have done in your situation, but I do want you to know that I'm very sorry and ask that you accept my apology. If you could find it in your heart, I'd be honored if you would accept my offer of friendship."

"Of course I accept your apology, Teddi. I knew that when I went in front of the church to announce I'd had a baby out of wedlock, it would probably end any hope I might have of forming friendships, and that it would certainly limit my opportunities for marriage to a good man. But I did it out of submission to God, and I knew He would be faithful to honor my obedience. Perhaps not in the way I would choose, but in ways that would even go beyond my expectations."

"And has He done that?" Teddi asked.

Margaret smiled a beautiful, broad smile that turned her already pretty face into a glorious work of beauty. "He just did," she said. "I almost stayed at home today, not wanting to sit on the sidelines watching while others enjoyed the pleasures of a winter afternoon skating. But something nudged me to quit feeling sorry for myself. And look what has happened!

I've made a new friend and also enjoyed a good portion of the afternoon skating with the most handsome young man in attendance."

"Thank you for your generous forgiveness," Teddi said, leaning forward and giving Margaret a hug. "One thing, however—my brother is *not* the most handsome man in attendance."

"I heard that," Jonathan retorted.

"You'd have to be deaf not to have heard it, brother. It was intended for your ears, also," Teddi replied. "It appears as though you've managed to convince Margaret, but I don't want you getting yourself all puffed up and proud, thinking that everybody agrees with her on that point."

The three of them were enjoying a good laugh when Phillip and Helen returned from skating and joined them, with Helen clinging to Phillip's arm and appearing surprised to see Margaret in their company.

"You three seem to be having a good time. I needed to warm up," he said, nearing the fire. "After I've gotten my circulation going again, would you care to join me on the ice, Teddi?" he asked.

"But I thought *we* were going to skate once you had warmed your hands," Helen complained to Phillip while giving Teddi a loathsome glare.

"I don't think we've been formally introduced," Phillip said, turning to Margaret.

Helen's irritation that she was being ignored was evident to all of them, yet she refused to loosen her hold on Phillip.

"I'm sorry. Phillip, this is Margaret Willoughby. Margaret, may I introduce you to Captain Phillip Hamilton, who is our new chaplain at Fort Riley," Teddi graciously replied.

"I'm pleased to meet you, Margaret," Phillip said, extending his right arm to shake Margaret's hand.

Unfortunately, Phillip's act of courtesy proved disastrous for Helen, who was still resolutely clinging to his arm and refused to let go when he extended his hand. The motion caused Helen to lose her balance, her arms and legs flying about pell-mell until she finally landed in a heap on the snow-covered ground in front of them.

"Look what you've done!" she screeched while looking directly at Margaret. "This is all *your* fault. Who invited you anyway?"

Phillip and Teddi gazed down at Helen, their faces etched with disbelief, while Jonathan rushed to Margaret's side.

"Phillip, help me up!" Helen commanded as she continued to glare at Margaret, who was now talking quietly to Jonathan.

"I'll help you to your feet, Helen, but that's all I intend to do," Phillip replied as he leaned down to help her up. "I'm shocked by your contemptuous attitude toward Margaret."

"You don't know anything about that woman. She's a harlot. In fact, she's even had a baby out of wedlock. You think that such a woman deserves to have her honor protected?" Helen spat.

"I don't know anything about her past, but I do know rude behavior when I see it. Good-bye, Helen," Phillip replied as he aided her and then turned away.

"Why don't we go skate for a while," Phillip said to the others. "Unless you'd rather leave?"

"We could skate a bit longer and then go back to our house for hot chocolate," Teddi suggested.

"That sounds like an excellent plan. What do you think, Margaret?"

"Me? Oh, I couldn't go to your home," she said in a throaty whisper.

"Why can't you? Are you expected home early?" Jonathan inquired.

"No, but perhaps you should discuss it with your parents, and then if they agree that it's all right, I'll come another time," she ventured.

"No need for that. Our friends are always welcome in our home," Teddi answered. "It will be fine, Margaret. You'll see. Please say you'll come with us," she encouraged.

Margaret nodded her agreement, and the four of them made their way onto the ice, the two couples skating off in opposite directions.

"I have a feeling there's more to this story than I've heard," Phillip remarked as he and Teddi glided toward the narrow portion of the creek where they had skated earlier in the afternoon.

"You're right, Phillip. And much of what I'm going to tell you may cause you to think that I'm not very different from Helen Hanson," she sadly related.

They moved up and down the ice, Teddi quietly telling Phillip of Margaret's confession and the brutal treatment she'd received since that time. At one point, Teddi noticed him wince at the words she was speaking, obviously pained by the shunning that Margaret had received from fellow Christians.

"I'm sure you find my behavior abhorrent," Teddi said as she concluded the ugly tale.

Phillip nodded his head in agreement. "Yes, I'm afraid I do. I'm sad that such a thing can happen, but I'm afraid that all too often, that's how we Christians treat one another. However, the difference between you and Helen is that you now realize the error of your ways and have asked God's forgiveness—and Margaret's," he added. "Perhaps your actions will begin to get things started down the right path with others. You've done a good thing today, Teddi," he said while squeezing her hand.

"Today I set things right, but when I think of all that Margaret has endured when I could have helped put an end to her suffering, I don't deserve her forgiveness," Teddi replied remorsefully.

"That may be true, but there's nothing you can do to

change the past. Instead of using valuable time worrying about the past, let's concentrate on what we can do to help Margaret in the future," Phillip suggested.

"You're right, of course," she said.

"It appears that Jonathan and Margaret are ready to leave," he said, pointing toward her brother and Margaret, who were now standing beside the sleigh.

By the time they had piled into the sleigh and were ready to head back home, only a few couples remained on the ice, and several of the men who had gathered around the fire were discussing how soon they should depart. Jonathan suggested that Teddi sit up front with Phillip and keep him company while he and Margaret sat in back. Giving her brother a knowing smile, she held out her hand and allowed Phillip to help her up beside him. The sun was beginning to set as Phillip pulled on the reins and a half-hour later brought the horses to a halt in front of the Yorke residence.

"Everybody out," he ordered as he jumped down, came around the sleigh, and assisted Teddi down.

"I told your father that you children would be home in time for supper," Isabelle announced as she pulled open the front door. "Didn't I, Clayton?" she asked, turning toward her husband.

"That you did, my dear. But, more importantly, you told Florence. Had you told only me of your belief, they would all go without supper since I've not yet learned to cook," he announced with a laugh.

"Where's George?" Isabelle asked while pointing at Jonathan's feet and motioning him toward the rug in front of the door.

"He went with Ruth Ann and some others that were heading into Junction City. They promised to bring him home. I thought he might already be here," Teddi replied.

"Well, if he went to Ruth Ann Langely's house, I'm sure

he's sitting down to supper right now. Kathryn Langely never misses an opportunity to have a guest for dinner. You children get your coats off and come in the parlor and warm up," Isabelle encouraged.

"I think you and Kathryn have a lot in common," General Yorke surmised as he gave his wife a broad grin.

Teddi noticed Isabelle's eyebrows rise after realizing it was Margaret Willoughby whom Jonathan had escorted home. Signaling her mother toward the kitchen, Teddi quickly recounted the day's events, told her mother she would answer any questions later, and graciously returned to the parlor with the report that dinner would soon be served.

Florence was at her culinary best, serving fried pork chops, mashed potatoes swimming in butter, and warm, flaky biscuits accompanied by her famous apple butter. After General Yorke gave thanks for the meal in his customary fashion, it became abundantly clear that the afternoon of skating had stimulated the appetites of the younger set, and, much to her delight, Florence was soon scurrying back to the kitchen to replenish the bowls and platters. Once their initial hunger had been appeased, their eating slowed to a normal pace, and the sounds of congenial conversation began to fill the room. Jonathan proudly announced that Margaret had mastered several new ice-skating maneuvers, and he was especially pleased to announce that she could now skate backwards.

Margaret soon joined in, acknowledging that she had been somewhat successful but confessing that her talents weren't nearly as admirable as Jonathan was boasting.

"After all, I did fall down four times and never did triumph totally unassisted. You *were* holding onto me," she admitted, giving Jonathan a sidelong glance.

"Success comes with patience and lots of practice, my dear," the general encouraged. "Jonathan will have to get you back on the ice soon. You'll be able to skate backwards unassisted in no time."

"Perhaps it's better that she doesn't learn *too* well, Father. I enjoy holding onto beautiful young ladies," Jonathan replied.

With the exception of Isabelle, who, Teddi decided, seemed somewhat distracted, their voices rose in laughter at Jonathan's comment. None of the others seemed to notice her mother's rather odd behavior until Isabelle, without warning, rose from the table and requested Teddi's assistance in the kitchen.

"Ring for Florence. You don't need to be running off to the kitchen when we have guests," the general stated as he motioned toward the small bell sitting by Isabelle's plate.

Isabelle complied and gave the bell a gentle shake, which caused Florence to hastily reappear.

"Yes, ma'am?" Florence questioned, wiping her wet hands on a cloth napkin.

"I was going to go to the kitchen and prepare coffee, but the general insisted that I remain at the table," she explained.

"But you always take your coffee in the parlor after dessert," Florence replied, her confusion evident.

"Well, I thought I'd do things differently this evening," Isabelle answered.

"So you want coffee now? Before I serve dessert?" Florence questioned.

"Oh, never mind. We'll have our coffee in the parlor after dessert, as usual. Well, I am permitted the privilege of changing my mind, aren't I?" she asked, obviously noticing the baffled look on Clayton's face.

"Of course, my dear. I'd never tell a woman she didn't have that privilege," he replied. "Now, then, what were we discussing? I believe you were telling me that you moved here when your father opened the dry goods store a year ago," the general continued, turning his attention back to

Margaret.

"That's what *you* were talking about, Father. I was going to ask Teddi to give me a list of dates and times for the holiday social activities in order to gain Margaret's assurance that she'll attend them all with me," Jonathan jovially interrupted.

"Well, I suppose that should take center stage," Clayton agreed. "Let's test your memory, Teddi. What's the social calendar look like for the next few weeks?"

"I'm not sure I can remember everything, but it's all written down in my journal. The next thing is the Hornbys' whist party on Tuesday, and then on Friday the party at Bert and Hannah's."

"Have the Mahoneys returned? That party may be canceled if they don't get back soon," Isabelle interjected while fidgeting with a small cameo brooch fastened to the collar of her dress.

"They got back yesterday," Clayton advised. "Bert said they had a good time, visited with relatives, and got some much-needed rest. Oh, he's brought another hunting dog back with him."

"And of course, there's the masked ball on Saturday," Teddi continued.

"Are you spoken for on those nights? I'd be proud to escort you to each of those parties. Please say yes," Jonathan implored a bewildered-appearing Margaret.

"She probably can't give you an answer right now, Jonathan. Besides, I thought you'd be escorting Teddi to the Christmas festivities," Isabelle replied before Margaret could speak.

"Why would Teddi want me as an escort when she can have Phillip?" Jonathan inquired, turning his full attention toward the beautiful, young woman at his side. "Have you agreed to attend with someone else?" he once again quizzed.

"No," Margaret answered softly.

"Then you'll allow me to escort you," he confidently

remarked.

"I suppose, if you really want to, and if your family doesn't mind," she murmured.

"Well, if we're going to take care of these matters right now, I suppose I'd better do the same. Teddi, may I have the honor of escorting *you?*" Phillip inquired.

"Why don't we discuss our arrangements later?" Teddi responded, sure that Phillip now felt required to invite her. But she wouldn't be anyone's obligatory date. She'd been attending social functions with her parents since Herbert's departure, and if her brother George wasn't available, she would continue to do so.

The logs in the dining-room fireplace had begun to turn an ashen white by the time Florence announced that coffee would be served in the parlor, *as usual.*

"I'm afraid my parents may begin to worry if I don't get home soon. Perhaps I could forego coffee?" Margaret inquired meekly.

"Of course! Clayton, why don't you see if one of your soldiers can take Margaret back to Junction City," Isabelle suggested to her husband.

As soon as the words had been spoken, a host of confused looks were once again cast in Isabelle's direction. A deafening silence filled the room until Jonathan gained his composure and spoke.

"Why would Father need to do that? Margaret is my guest, so I'll be escorting her home. Mind if I use your sleigh, Phillip?"

"Not at all. I'll walk back to my quarters, and you can have the privilege of caring for the horses upon your return," Phillip replied in a lighthearted voice as the group rose from the table.

ten

"What *were* you thinking, Mother?" Teddi inquired after Phillip had bid them good night, and Clayton had excused himself to go over some paperwork upstairs.

Isabelle didn't lift her eyes from the piece of embroidery work upon which she was carefully stitching. "I thought that Margaret should probably ask her parents before accepting Jonathan's invitations," Isabelle replied.

"No, mother, I'm inquiring about *everything*. Why did you treat Margaret so rudely, suggesting that one of the soldiers take her home and making it obvious you didn't want her to accept Jonathan's invitations? Why, you didn't have one kind thing to say to her all evening. I'm shocked at your behavior, especially after what I told you in the kitchen," Teddi angrily replied.

"It's one thing to forgive her past mistakes, Teddi. But I don't want your brother keeping company with her. What if he should fall in love with Margaret and want to marry her?" Isabelle asked, putting her sewing aside to give Teddi her full attention. "It could have a lasting impact on his personal life as well as his career. Right or wrong, I want the very best spouses for my children, and I don't think Margaret falls into that category."

"You thought Herbert Albright was an excellent choice for me, and look what happened there," Teddi countered. "And is it truly forgiveness when there are exceptions such as those you're imposing, Mother? What if Jesus had placed such limitations on His forgiveness?"

"I want to discuss this with Jonathan as well as your father.

I'm sure neither of them knows anything about—"

"Knows anything about what?" Jonathan asked as he walked in the front door. Stomping the snow off his feet with great bravado, he pulled off his overcoat and walked into the parlor, immediately making his way to stand in front of the fireplace.

"We were having a private conversation," Isabelle replied.

"Well, I heard you say that you wanted to discuss something with me. Here I am," he said, giving her a winsome smile. "So let's discuss!"

Isabelle looked as though she wanted to flee from the room, but there appeared to be no escape. Jonathan was wide awake after being out in the cold, late-night air, and Teddi had settled back into her chair with her hands folded in her lap, awaiting her mother's opening remarks.

Isabelle absently picked up her sewing and began making tiny satin stitches, the needle moving in and out of the piece of fabric at breakneck speed. She cleared her throat several times and then, while keeping her gaze focused on the sewing, began to question her son's earlier decisions.

Teddi watched her brother stiffen as Isabelle began recounting the events of Margaret's past, his irritation growing more and more evident as Isabelle continued her speech while never once raising her eyes. Finally, Jonathan took three long steps to where his mother was sitting and stood directly in front of her.

"Why won't you look at me, Mother? Do you find what you're saying so embarrassing that you can't meet my eyes, or is it that you know you're wrong, and I would see the deceit if you met my gaze?"

Isabelle's head snapped upward at his remark, her face now filled with anger. "Can't you see that I'm trying to protect you from a future of misery and shame? I don't dislike Margaret. I suppose making her confession in front of the congregation was commendable, although I'm not convinced it showed good judgment. And I'm certain her parents would have preferred that she remain silent about her past. All of that happened before she moved to Junction City, so I'm not sure why she felt it was necessary to make it known. It's almost as though she's proud of having had a child and giving it up."

Jonathan dropped onto the sofa across the room from the two women. "I can't believe this is my mother speaking. Margaret was very honest with me. We hadn't even circled the ice when she told me all the things you've recounted. Perhaps she wouldn't have felt it necessary to do that if people around here had truly forgiven her. I knew all of those things before I invited her to be my guest, and I'll be proud to escort her.

"There are things in my past that I'm not proud of either. But I didn't have Margaret's courage. I merely confessed my sins to God and asked His forgiveness, rather than that of my fellow man. We're a strange lot, we humans, feeling rather smug with our deep, dark secrets privately tucked away from the world. But let one brave soul come forward, making public a past failure and begging our forgiveness, and what do we do? We pay lip service to their courage, tell them all is forgiven, and then politely ignore the fact that they exist. Quite noble, don't you think?"

"I know my feelings are unjustified, but. . ."

"But what, Mother? Your statements are in total opposition to the Bible's teachings. There is no justification for that, and I've never known you to defy the Word of God. Is the opinion of other people so important to you?"

Isabelle rose, placed her sewing in the basket near her chair, and turned her tear-filled gaze upon Jonathan. "I need to pray about this," she said as she turned to leave the room. Her shoulders were slumped and her gait slow and measured as she walked to the staircase and made her way up the steps.

"*You* don't agree with her, do you?" Jonathan asked, quickly turning his attention toward his sister.

"No. In fact, I had been questioning her behavior toward Margaret before you returned home. She's trying to protect you, Jonathan. I know, I know," she said, holding up her hand to stave off his interruption. "You don't need protection. But parents don't quit doing that just because their children reach a certain age or leave home. Trust her when she says she'll pray about it, Jonathan. She will! And I am certain she'll receive clarity on the issue. I can't completely condemn her because I haven't treated Margaret any more civilly than the rest of the community," Teddi replied. "Come on—we'd better get to bed."

"I'm not tired. I think I'll wait for George," he answered. "Any of Florence's pie left in the kitchen?"

"Of course, and I'm sure you'll be able to find it without much difficulty. Good night, Jonathan," she said, rising up on her toes to kiss him on the cheek.

"Thanks for your support with this whole thing. Margaret is a wonderful girl, and I don't intend to lose her," Jonathan replied.

"And beautiful, too," Teddi added.

"*Very* beautiful," he responded.

"And that's the most important thing," she muttered to herself while walking up the stairway to her bedroom.

❧

Phillip had been at the hospital only a short time when he heard the front door open. Jumping from his chair, he turned for a moment as the anatomy book he'd been reading went tumbling to the floor with a resolute thud. Leaning down, he grabbed the book, threw it back onto his desk, and rushed to the vestibule. Teddi had just arrived, the bottom of her long, woolen coat covered with a dusting of snow that was beginning to melt and drip onto the small rug at the entryway.

Moving with a long, determined stride, he reached out to assist her as she removed her coat.

"Thank you, Phillip," she said with a look of amusement on her face as she hung the coat, careful to ensure that the melting snow would fall upon the small, braided rug.

"You're smiling. Did I miss something amusing?" he inquired.

"No. I'm just not used to having help with my coat. I'm sure you have much more important things to do."

"Not at the moment. I wanted to have our discussion this morning before we got too busy. Why don't you come into my office?" he offered.

"Our discussion?"

"Yes. Last night you said we would discuss our arrangements later—about my escorting you to the upcoming social events. Several of the parties are only a few days off, so I thought we should probably—"

"Have our chat so you have time to make other arrangements once I've freed you from your obligation to escort me," Teddi interrupted.

"What? I *don't* feel obligated, as you so ineptly put it. I would consider it a privilege to have you on my arm. I thought we would be making arrangements about the times and dates, not about whether we were actually going to attend the parties as a couple."

"You expect me to believe that you intended to invite me before my brother made his ill-spoken remark at dinner last night?" she asked, giving him an incredulous look.

"Yes. Why would you find that so hard to believe?"

"Let's see. Perhaps it's because you couldn't keep your eyes off Helen Hanson at the cast party. Or perhaps it's because you were completely infatuated by her beauty and charm at the skating party, until she offended you with her

treatment of Margaret. I think you'd be happier with someone whose appearance you find more pleasing, and wearing
a gown isn't going to change me into a beauty," she candidly
answered.

"I'll not deny that initially my head was turned by her
beauty. But it didn't take long for me to realize that she's a
shallow, vain, young lady and that we have nothing in common. I apologize for my behavior and promise that it won't
happen again if you'll agree to accompany me. Don't I get a
second chance?" he asked, giving her a doleful look.

"I suppose we all deserve at least a second chance," she
agreed, giving him a halfhearted smile. "You can call for me
at eight o'clock on Thursday evening."

"What about Friday and Saturday?" he quickly interjected.

"Let's see how Thursday goes."

"But if everything goes well and you have a pleasant
evening, you'll accompany me on Friday and Saturday?" he
pursued.

Teddi leaned forward in the chair and gave him a grin. "If
we have an agreeable evening, and if you still want to escort
me on Friday and Saturday, then the answer would be yes,"
she conceded.

"Wonderful!" he whooped, bounding out of his chair.
"Now that we've gotten that settled, let's get to the ward and
begin seeing our patients."

As they worked side by side during the succeeding days,
Phillip determined Teddi was beginning to trust him a little
more. She appeared more relaxed in his company, and she didn't
hesitate to ask for his assistance when a problem arose with
one of the patients. There were more patients in the hospital
than Phillip had anticipated, but with all of the men garrisoned
at the post for the winter, he assumed the increased number of
patients was to be expected. It would have been impossible to
care for all of them without Teddi's capable assistance. She

ensured that the soldiers working in the hospital were trained and skilled in their duties, and if they didn't meet her standards, she asked that they be reassigned outside the hospital. There was no doubt that Teddi's first concern was the care and well-being of the patients. She had even mentioned planting a vegetable garden outside the hospital again this year, and Phillip took that as a favorable sign. At least she was planning to continue working at the hospital.

And yesterday she had completely surprised him by asking when he planned on beginning the Bible study, suggesting several topics she thought might interest the young adults. Her ideas had been sound, and it pleased him that she was giving positive consideration to some of his suggestions for the chapel.

By Thursday, Phillip was looking forward to spending the evening with Teddi. "I'll be at your quarters by eight o'clock," he said as they were leaving the hospital.

"We should probably leave a little earlier. Jonathan will need to stop at Margaret's home in Junction City before going on to the Hornbys'. Will that be a problem?" she asked.

"No, not at all. I'll be there at seven-thirty. The more time together, the better, as far as I'm concerned," he replied with a broad smile.

He watched until Teddi was out of sight and then walked back to his quarters. Phillip had decided to wear one of his two civilian suits to the party. Both were quite stylish, and since he was required to wear his uniform to all military galas, it seemed the party in Junction City would provide him with an opportunity to blend in with the rest of the town's residents. Besides, he reasoned, being out of his military uniform might cause Teddi to view him as more of an admirer than the doctor or chaplain she worked with at the hospital.

❧

Straightening his tie, Phillip rushed up the front stairs to the

Yorke residence and knocked on the door. General Yorke pulled open the door but appeared startled when he saw Phillip standing before him in a black greatcoat, which remained unbuttoned and permitted a view of his gray double-breasted jacket, waistcoat, and trousers. A gray silk tie was neatly fastened around his starched, white collar, and a pair of shiny leather oxfords had replaced his black military boots. He quickly removed the black, silk top hat when the general motioned him inside.

"Surprised to see you in that getup," the general remarked as he gave Phillip a slap on the back. "Tired of the uniform already?"

"No, sir. Just thought it might be a nice change," Phillip replied.

"Women prefer men in uniforms, you know," he said with a boisterous laugh.

"Well, I'm not looking to impress anyone but Teddi, so I hope she doesn't mind," he said just as Teddi descended the stairs.

"He looks very handsome in civilian clothing, Father. Besides, I think that it was probably a soldier who decided women prefer men in uniform," she said with a smile.

"Possibly. But there are a lot of military wives who agree with me. Where's your brother?"

"Right here, Father," Jonathan replied as he came down the steps two at a time. "You're going to put me to shame," he said to Phillip, pulling back the overcoat to gain a better view of Phillip's suit.

"I doubt anyone is going to be interested in what we're wearing. It's always the ladies' dresses that everyone's interested in. Speaking of which, that's a lovely gown you're wearing," he said to Teddi.

"Thank you, Phillip. We'd better be going or they'll start without us. Don't wait up, Father," she instructed, leaning over to place a kiss on his cheek.

"Have a good time, but don't forget that tomorrow's a working day, and there's a party tomorrow night, too. Best not stay out too late."

Ella Hornby was beginning to arrange people at the tables just as the foursome arrived. Mrs. Hornby greeted them, took their wraps, and instructed them to join the others in the parlor. They each dropped a calling card in the silver tray that was placed in the center of a claw-footed oak table in the entryway. Phillip breathed a sigh of relief when Mrs. Hornby didn't appear disturbed by Margaret's appearance at the party.

"Hurry up—I've already placed your names in the drawing," Ella told them as they entered the room.

"Drawing for what?" Jonathan inquired.

"To see where we'll be seated to play whist. I've divided the ladies' and gentlemen's names into separate bowls. I'll draw two from each bowl, and those four people will play at the first table, and so on," Ella explained.

"I want to sit with Margaret," Jonathan whispered at Teddi.

"It's not my party. You'll have to go along with it."

Phillip was pleased when Ella drew Margaret's name and she was seated at the same table as Jonathan. But when the drawing was completed, Teddi was seated across the room with Ella and two fellows who had attended the skating party, while Phillip ended up with Helen Hanson, Mattie Fielding, and William Hornby.

Phillip saw Teddi glance in his direction just as Helen placed her hand over his and gave it a squeeze.

"I need to talk with you. It's very important," Helen whispered with a note of urgency, her breath tickling his ear as she spoke.

"Talk away. You have my undivided attention," he replied, beginning to shuffle the cards.

"Not here. It's a private matter. When we change tables,

we always mingle and have refreshments. We'll talk then," she quietly replied.

It had been several years since Phillip had played whist, but the game soon came back to him. In fact, he and Mattie managed to soundly defeat Helen and William. However, Helen was playing so poorly that it gave him cause to wonder if she didn't understand the game or if she was intentionally misplaying her cards. Poor William seemed totally unnerved by her lack of skill, and when the game was finally over, he vaulted out of his chair to the refreshment table without saying a word.

"Could you give us a few minutes alone, Mattie?" Helen purred.

Mattie jumped at her cue and rushed off to join William at the refreshment table. None of the others had completed their game, and Helen took the opportunity to move her chair closer to Phillip. Once again she leaned over and began whispering, occasionally leaning back to emit a soft giggle or murmur some remark loud enough for the others to hear. Her performance didn't go unnoticed.

Finally, when the last group had completed their game, Ella announced they would adjourn to the dining room for refreshments before beginning the next game. Phillip immediately rose from the table, only to feel Helen's fingers winding around his arm, digging into his flesh with a viselike grip. As he attempted to free his arm, Teddi turned toward them, watching as Helen giggled. When Phillip asked her to release his arm, instead she shrewdly placed her head on his shoulder for a moment and gave him an engaging smile.

"Teddi," he called out, finally wresting his arm out of Helen's grip and crossing the room.

"Feel free to join Helen at the refreshment table. I can find my own way," Teddi snapped.

"I don't want to join Helen. I didn't ask to sit with her and

I can't control her behavior. She said she had something she needed to discuss with me as soon as I was seated at the table," he explained.

"I see. And the only way she could talk to you was by putting her lips up against your ear? Quite frankly, Phillip, I didn't see you objecting to her attention," Teddi stated. "If you'll excuse me, I'm going to get a cup of cocoa and something to eat."

Phillip stood in stunned silence as Teddi marched off, leaving him to his own devices. Before he could decide how to handle the situation, Helen was back from the refreshment table carrying two plates laden with tasty treats.

"I brought you a plate, and I have something else I want to tell you," Helen said as she settled in beside him. "I apologized to Margaret for my bad behavior the other day." There was a look of pride on her face, and she stared at Phillip as if she expected some sort of enthusiastic reply.

"That's wonderful, Helen, if your apology was genuine and not given to serve some ulterior purpose," Phillip said.

"Well, of course it was genuine, Phillip. Why would you doubt my intentions?" she asked while giving him an exaggerated pout.

"If you'll excuse me, I see someone I want to speak to," Phillip said in an attempt to get away from her. "Jonathan!" he called, quickly moving toward his friend.

Jonathan turned and gave him a smile. He and Margaret seemed to be enjoying themselves, and as far as he could tell, the other guests were including Margaret in their conversation.

"Where's Teddi?" Jonathan inquired, looking about the room.

"It appears I've offended her—again," Phillip answered. "Do you think you could speak to her and help me straighten this out?"

"I can try. What happened?"

Phillip gave his friend a quick explanation and sent him off in search of Teddi while he remained close by Margaret's side. He wanted to protect Margaret from any ungracious behavior that might occur in Jonathan's absence, but he also hoped that her presence would keep Helen at arm's length.

"I understand Helen apologized," Phillip quietly remarked as they stood at the far end of the dining room.

Margaret gave him a faint smile and nodded her head ever so slightly. "I suppose you could call it that."

"Was she unkind?"

"Helen's apology is of little consequence to me. She's not someone I would choose as a friend, so it makes no difference. I'd rather talk about something more pleasant," she answered.

Phillip honored her wishes and quickly changed the subject, but he was now sure that Helen had merely added insult to injury with her so-called apology. They were discussing the upcoming masquerade ball when Teddi and Jonathan approached. Phillip breathed a sigh of relief when Teddi smiled and moved next to him.

"Have you had refreshments?" she asked.

"Yes, Helen. . ." He wanted to choke back her name, but he couldn't. It was hanging in midair, separating them, just as immovably as if she'd physically walked between them.

Teddi finally broke the thick silence. "You and Helen ate together?"

"Not exactly. She went and filled a plate and brought it to me. I certainly didn't ask her to do such a thing, and I never expected it. She just appeared with two plates of food and sat down beside me. Teddi, I don't want to spend the evening with that woman. I don't know how to make you believe me. Surely you realize that I had no control over the seating arrangements."

"Yes, Phillip, I do understand what occurred. Let's go back into the parlor."

When Ella announced that the guests could choose the partner of their choice for the remainder of the games, Phillip quickly asked Teddi. He hoped that her agreement was a sign that the earlier events of the evening had been forgotten.

eleven

At her mother's insistence, Teddi had been working on her costume for the masquerade ball for several months. Now, she was pleased that it had been completed and was hanging in the closet awaiting the party. There were a number of guests who had failed to appear at the Mahoneys' due to last-minute stitching on costumes, among them Helen Hanson.

Helen's failure to appear at that get-together had permitted Teddi to relax and enjoy the evening's festivities. The game of charades had been great fun, and she'd been amazed by Phillip's clever performances. He had proved to be good at both acting out his clues as well as guessing the actions of others who were performing. In fact, their team had been in total agreement that, without Phillip, they would never have won.

Although she had all but begged him to tell, Phillip had steadfastly refused to divulge what he would be wearing when he came to call on her this evening. Many of the married couples wore outfits that complemented each other, but those who were single most often decided upon a costume without consulting their escorts.

Phillip had agreed to help Jonathan and George find costumes among the wardrobe stored for use by the theater troupe. Isabelle had been delighted to have that task removed from her list of worries and promised Phillip Sunday dinner for the rest of the year. She had, however, been somewhat embarrassed when Phillip pointed out the fact that there were only two Sundays left until the beginning of the new year and that he hoped she would consider an extension.

"Are you absolutely positive that you don't want to tell me

what you'll be wearing this evening?" Teddi asked as she was leaving the hospital for the day.

"Of course not! That's half the fun. I want to see if you'll be able to find me in the crowd."

As was the custom, Teddi would go to the ball with her family. Then, after everyone had arrived, the partygoers would begin to seek out their escorts. Inevitably there were occasions when couples would go through most of the evening thinking they'd found their escort, only to be surprised when the masks came off. Although the use of accents to disguise voices was commonplace on masquerade night, Teddi was certain she'd have no difficulty detecting Phillip.

Jonathan insisted he was not going to attend with the family and had already left for Junction City to get Margaret. Teddi wasn't sure if it was because he feared the possibility Margaret might suffer insult from someone attending the party, or if he was unwilling to spend any part of the evening with other girls while he attempted to find her. Either way, Margaret had agreed to the arrangement. And surprisingly, Isabelle had remained silent on the issue.

"Do you need any help with your costume, Teddi?" Isabelle asked as she tapped on Teddi's bedroom door.

"No, I think I'm ready. Come in and see what you think."

"It's lovely, and such a unique idea. I don't think you need worry about anyone else duplicating your costume. Come along. I believe your father is waiting impatiently at the bottom of the stairs."

"You look beautiful, Mother," Teddi remarked as they walked down the hallway. "Do you feel like you're getting married all over again?"

"Not quite, but it does please me that I can still wear my wedding dress. Especially since I had to let out all the seams in your father's suit," she said, causing both women to laugh.

"What's so funny?" Clayton asked as mother and daughter

walked down the steps.

"Just reminiscing, dear," was all that Isabelle said.

"Well, now, that certainly takes me back," Clayton said as he twirled Isabelle around in the parlor. "My bride has returned after all these years, looking even more beautiful, if that's possible," he complimented. "And, you, Teddi, aren't you just gorgeous? I would have never known it was you. What a remarkable costume!"

"Where's George?" Isabelle inquired. "We need to be on our way."

"He decided to ride along with Jonathan, so it's just the three of us."

"Don't forget, we're going to the theater building, not the mess hall," Isabelle instructed as Clayton helped them into the sleigh.

Clayton gave her one of his uncontrolled laughs, his beefy cheeks puffing the cold night air. "I think I can remember where we're going. My mind isn't quite that bad yet, my dear."

"I wasn't insulting your memory, Clayton, but the masquerade ball has been at the dining hall ever since we've been at Fort Riley. With all the important things you have to remember, I didn't know if you might overlook something so trivial."

"That was an excellent piece of diplomacy," he said, kissing his wife on the cheek.

"We're off," he called out into the cold night air. "To the theater," he added, and then he graced them with another hearty laugh.

The theater was ablaze with light when they arrived amid guests alighting from sleighs that in many cases sat some distance away from the front door.

"I'll let you ladies out here and go put the sleigh in back," Clayton instructed. "Go on inside, and I'll be with you momentarily."

"I've never seen so many people at this ball," Teddi said to her mother.

"The Junction City newspaper printed several excellent articles about the event and encouraged everyone to attend. And the theater has enough room for them all," Isabelle replied.

The stage curtain had been raised, and the stage would be their dance floor for the evening. Barry's Band from Junction City was in the pit providing music, and many of the theater chairs had been removed to allow the guests extra room to mingle. Large banquet tables were covered with linen cloths and decorated with greenery and candles, and festive, red bows festooned the rough-hewn support beams throughout the building.

"Oh, look, there's Jonathan. He must have told Margaret what he would be wearing. Their costumes match. Folks will think they're a married couple," Teddi remarked as she moved toward them. "Jonathan!" she called, waving her arm.

"Don't you look quite stunning," Jonathan remarked. "Where did you ever come up with the idea of dressing like a rainbow?"

"I don't know. I think they're beautiful and decided I could make a dress and accessories that would resemble a rainbow."

"And so you have. It is truly beautiful," Margaret replied. "Here we are dressed as hobos, looking quite destitute while you look stunning."

"I don't think I could ever look stunning, Margaret, but thank you for your kind words. I haven't spotted Phillip. What is he wearing, Jonathan?"

"I don't know. He wouldn't tell me—said he was sure you could wheedle it out of me if he told. He's probably right!"

"He truly didn't tell you? But I was depending on you, Jonathan. Look how many people are in this place! How am I ever going to find him?"

"I suppose like everyone else. Accept dance invitations and

talk to everyone you can. You'd best get started mingling; we're off to the dance floor. Now you see why I didn't want to come without Margaret on my arm," he said with a laugh.

In the past, attending with her family had never been a problem. Their first year at Fort Riley, she didn't have an escort; after that, Herbert had always told her in advance what he would be wearing. If she had known there would be so many guests, she would have insisted Phillip divulge his costume.

"May I have this dance, lassie?"

Teddi looked at a man attired in a gray-and-red-plaid Irish kilt, a white shirt, gray wool waistcoat, and red kneesocks. She didn't think it was Phillip, yet there was something strangely familiar about him. He was disguising his voice with a pronounced Irish accent. Perhaps once they were on the dance floor, she'd be able to tell for sure.

"My, but you're lookin' lovely tonight, lassie," he said as they twirled across the wooden boards. "And you feel just right in my arms, I might add."

"Phillip?" she asked.

"You can call me by any name you like, so long as you promise to spend your time with me," he replied.

His hands! That would let her know for sure. But as soon as the thought raced through her mind, she felt the cloth of his gloved hand. He'd even thought to cover his hands. It must be Phillip, for he'd expect her to look at his hands. Yet something wasn't quite right.

"Do I have the promise of all your dances, lassie?" he asked as the music ceased playing.

"Not yet. I'm not sure you're Phillip," she replied. "I'd better wait until I've danced with some other gentlemen."

"I'll be here waitin' for you, lassie. You're the one I came for, and you're the one I'll have," he said while escorting her off the stage.

Before she had time to give further consideration to the Irishman, a pirate was walking her back to the stage. However, they had taken only a few dance steps when she was sure the pirate wasn't Phillip. She giggled when the pirate kept forgetting his pirate jargon and slipped back into using his own voice.

She moved through dance after dance while the Irishman continued to stand by the stage and watch her, never leaving his post.

"Have time for a dance with your father?" Clayton asked.

"Of course," Teddi replied, taking his hand and walking onto the makeshift dance floor. "Have you seen Phillip?" she asked once the music had begun.

"No, can't say as I have. Of course, I haven't figured out who much of anybody is. I take it you're having trouble finding him."

"I'm not sure. The first person who asked me to dance is that man dressed like an Irishman standing by the stage. He seems so familiar, yet I'm not positive it's Phillip. When I asked him if he was Phillip, he said I could call him by any name I liked as long as I spent my time with him," she explained.

"If you don't know of another gentleman who might want to spend the evening with you, I'd say it's probably Phillip. That man looks to be the same size and height as Phillip. Did you ask Jonathan?"

"Phillip wouldn't even tell him what he was wearing. He said I could probably wheedle it out of Jonathan."

The general gave an uproarious laugh. "I'd say Phillip knows you pretty well! Why don't you dance a couple more dances with the Irishman? Then maybe you'll be sure," he suggested as they left the floor.

She nodded her head, and General Yorke led her off the floor toward where the man stood watching them.

"Good evening, General Yorke. I hope you're bringing

your lovely lassie to dance with me," the Irishman said with his thick accent.

"I think perhaps I am," Clayton said, handing Teddi over.

"I've decided I need to dance with you again in order to be sure you're the man I want to spend my evening with," she told him.

"Ah, Lassie, not only am I the man you want to spend the evening with, but I'm also the man you'll be spending your life with," he confidently replied.

Teddi was surprised by the comment. Obviously Phillip felt much more assured of their relationship when hidden behind a mask and Irish brogue.

≈

Phillip surveyed the crowd. He knew Teddi wouldn't stay close by her parents, but he had felt an assurance he'd be able to find her. Jonathan had even volunteered to ask what she'd be wearing, but Phillip had declined the offer. Just as he was becoming a bit concerned, he was certain that he now spotted her. There was no doubt it was Teddi, although he was surprised she hadn't taken greater pains to hide her identity.

"So you did recognize me. I told Jonathan I was sure I'd be able to fool you," Phillip said as he approached her. "I could have picked you out anywhere. That's a beautiful costume," he added, relishing her portrayal of a Southern belle as she twirled a fancy parasol above her head.

"Why, thank you, kind sir," she replied, giving him a deep curtsy while feigning a Southern accent.

"You don't need to use that accent, Teddi; I know it's you," Phillip replied, lifting the side of his mask and allowing her a peek. "I told you I'd reveal myself if you found me," he continued.

"I've decided I rather like my Southern drawl. By the way, how did you know it was me? Now, that was a silly question, wasn't it? All these tiny-waisted girls, and then there's me."

"Don't talk about yourself in such a manner, Teddi. You are a lovely, young woman, and I admire you very much. It hurts me when you speak poorly of yourself. If it were only appearances that interested me, I'd be searching out someone like Helen Hanson. I thought you understood that what I'm seeking in a wife is someone with your attributes. Beauty isn't merely someone's outer appearance; it's who that person is inside," Phillip replied.

"Let's don't talk anymore, Phillip. Let's enjoy the music and dance."

They finished the set without so much as a word passing between them, although he was pleased when she squeezed his hand several times and placed her head on his shoulder.

"Why don't we get some punch?" Phillip asked as the music stopped.

"I'm quite warm. Could we go outside?"

"It's freezing out there. You'd catch your death of cold," Phillip warned.

"We could sit under the buffalo robe in your sleigh and talk for awhile. There are some things I want to discuss with you, and it's noisy in here. I'm sure I'd be able to keep warm there," she said, the words dripping with her Southern drawl.

"I suppose, if you really want to," he hesitantly agreed, though surprised by her request.

ᥲ

"Teddi, my love, you've brought me such joy this fine evening. I have a very important question I want to ask you before the night has ended," the Irishman whispered in her ear.

A tingling sensation coursed down her spine with each word that he spoke, and his lips lightly brushed her neck in the slightest hint of a kiss as he pulled her closer. She squeezed his hand in her own, unable to restrain the love that had begun to well up inside her weeks ago. Not that she wanted this to happen so quickly. After Herbert, she had never wanted to love again. But Phillip's kindness and concern, his gentle acceptance of her, and his sweet words whispered in her ear dissolved all her defenses. Phillip was an honorable man who would be a good husband to her and a good father to her children. There was no reason why she shouldn't love him.

"Would you like something cool to drink?"

"Yes, thank you," she replied, following him to the refreshment table.

He filled two cups and handed her one. "Follow me. There's a quiet place where we can talk back here."

"In one of the dressing rooms? I don't know if we should," she stammered.

"Trust me, Lassie," he said, pulling her along beside him until they reached the hallway.

The hallway behind the stage was narrow, causing Teddi to follow along behind. The man held her hand tightly as he opened the door and pulled her inside. The door closed behind them and the room was dark and silent. She felt his hands touch her face as he slowly lifted her mask and ran his finger ever so lightly across her lips. She could hear his shallow breathing as his face lowered toward hers, his mouth seeking and then covering her own in a lingering kiss.

"Phillip, we need to go back to the party," Teddi urged as their lips parted.

"Say that you'll marry me," he demanded, still using his Irish accent as he pulled her tightly against him. "Give me your promise, or I'll keep you here until you do, lassie."

His lips once again found hers, and she yielded to the tenderness of his kiss. "Yes, I'll marry you," she whispered. "I promise."

twelve

General Yorke pulled off his shoes and leaned back in his favorite chair, wishing he'd have pulled the seat a bit closer to the fireplace, yet too weary to get up and move it. Isabelle came fluttering in from the kitchen, still wearing her wedding dress, carrying a pan filled with warm water.

"Give me a pair of leather cavalry boots over these fandangled gentlemen's slippers any day of the week," the general complained as he rolled up his trousers, pulled off his socks, and tentatively placed his big toe in the water.

"It's not hot. You act as though I'm going to scald you," Isabelle remarked.

"Just checking. It's bad enough having these blisters; I don't want burns on my feet, too. I wouldn't be able to walk at all," he complained.

"Good heavens, Clayton, what are you going to do if you ever have a serious medical problem?" Isabelle retorted. "I'm going upstairs to get out of this dress. I'll be down and see how you're doing in a few minutes."

She had made it to the first landing when the front door burst open and Teddi rushed into the house, the Irishman following close on her heels.

"Why did you leave without me?" she asked in an accusatory tone.

"Your father said you'd come home with Phillip. Oh, oh," Isabelle gasped. "Where did *you* come from?"

"What's going on out there?" General Yorke called from the parlor.

"Good evening, General. I wanted to come in with Teddi to

115

tell you the good news. She's given her promise to marry me!"

"What? She would never give her promise to marry you, Albright. Teddi, what's he talking about, and what is he doing in this house?"

"Herbert is the Irishman, Father. He pretended to be Phillip and asked me to marry him," Teddi answered, tears streaming down her face. "After the two of you left, he went about telling all the guests that we were going to be married. I denied it, but he kept telling people I was only jesting, that we were truly to be married, and that I had forgiven his outrageous behavior."

The sight of Herbert Albright had caused Isabelle to visibly pale, but her faintness soon gave way to anger. "How dare you humiliate our daughter again! What are you up to? You're already a married man. Why would you do such a thing?"

"Alas, my wife succumbed to cholera out on the prairie," he replied with theatrical flair. "Had she lived, the marriage wouldn't have lasted. She knew my heart remained with Teddi."

"You unfeeling cad! I want you out of this house and out of my life," Teddi cried.

"I'll leave for now, but I'm sure you'll come around. I'll be staying in Junction City for the next month, so we'll be seeing each other at all the socials. In fact, I'll just plan on being your escort."

"Get out of here! I would rather *die* than be seen with you," she screeched.

"You may change your mind, so let's keep the option available. After all, you don't know where Phillip was spending his time this evening, do you?" he asked as he left the house.

"Oh, Mother, what if someone told Phillip that I've pledged myself to Herbert again? How could this happen?"

"We need to remain calm and keep our wits, or none of us will be able to think," Isabelle replied. "Did you ever see Phillip?"

"No, I thought Herbert was Phillip. He used that foolish accent all evening. I kept sensing a familiarity about him and thought it must be Phillip. I asked both Jonathan and George throughout the evening, but both of them denied ever seeing him. Maybe he's ill and didn't go at all. Oh, I hope that's what happened," Teddi said, the thought giving her a glimmer of hope. If Phillip hadn't attended the party, she could explain everything before he heard the lies from others.

"Nothing's going to be settled by sitting up all night. Besides, this water is getting cold," the general stated as he pulled his feet out of the water.

Teddi went upstairs and readied herself for bed, but instead of crawling beneath the covers, she paced back and forth until her father finally knocked on the wall and told her to get in bed. Later, when she heard Jonathan come home, she considered running downstairs to talk with him. But she would have awakened at least one of her parents and suffered their wrath, so she reluctantly turned over and stared at the wall, finally falling asleep shortly before dawn.

A tapping at her bedroom door awakened her only a few hours after she had fallen asleep. "You need to get up, Teddi, or we'll be late for church."

Church! She'd see Phillip at church, but in all likelihood he'd already have heard about last night's happenings before she arrived. The thought of seeing all those people, having them stare and whisper behind their hands, watching them give each other knowing smiles, made her want to plow back under the covers and remain there for the rest of her life.

"I'm not sure I can go to church this morning, Mother."

"Are you ill?" her mother questioned.

"Not exactly. But I will be if I'm forced to face all those gossips," Teddi replied.

"The longer you hide behind closed doors, the harder it will be to face the world. Get out of bed and get ready. We're going to church!" Isabelle responded firmly.

Teddi pulled out a dark brown dress with pleated sleeves and tan decorative lapels. Both the skirt and lapels were adorned with matching, gold buttons. Looking into the mirror, she donned her dark brown hat that sported tan and brown feathers, and snugly tied it under her chin.

"Come have some breakfast before we leave," her mother urged.

"Where are Jonathan and George?" Teddi asked, surveying the room. She wanted them close at hand in case she felt the need to make a quick getaway.

"I'm not sure. They were up early and have already left," Isabelle said. "Hurry now!"

Untying her hat and placing it on a table in the living room, Teddi hesitantly filled her plate and sat down at the table; however, eating proved impossible. She chased her scrambled eggs around the plate and nibbled on one of Florence's muffins, but her stomach rebelled, so she finally quit trying.

"You ladies ready?" Clayton asked as he came in the front door. "I've got the sleigh waiting."

"We'll get our coats and be with you in just a moment," Isabelle replied.

"I'd really prefer to stay home," Teddi said, remaining in her chair.

"You're not staying home. Don't forget we'll have extra guests for dinner, Florence," Isabelle called out toward the kitchen.

"Oh, that's right. You invited Phillip to dinner."

"And Margaret, plus both of your brothers, and I believe George invited Ruth Ann. We should have quite a roomful."

"Wonderful," Teddi replied dejectedly.

"That didn't sound very enthusiastic. Don't borrow trouble, Teddi—everything may turn out just fine."

"I know, Mother. 'Do not worry about tomorrow, for tomorrow will worry about itself. Each day has enough trouble of its own.' I've been repeating that verse quite a bit lately," Teddi replied as they walked out the door.

The ride to church came to a halt much too soon for Teddi, but she gathered her courage and stepped into the limestone chapel, with her parents following close behind. Jonathan, Margaret, Ruth Ann, and George were already seated in the Yorkes' regular pew. Teddi slid in beside Ruth Ann and turned her attention to the front of the church. Phillip was busy leafing through his Bible, and if he ever attempted to look in her direction, she missed it when someone tapped her on the shoulder.

Glancing to the row behind her, Teddi found herself eye to eye with Herbert, who was looking far too smug to suit her. Ignoring his grin, she turned around and faced forward. She wanted to tell her mother Herbert was seated behind them, but she knew he would be delighted if she did anything that indicated he was making her uncomfortable. She was surprised to see Helen Hanson and her friend Mattie seated across the aisle. They were both members of a church in Junction City, and Teddi couldn't remember ever seeing them at the post chapel before. Obviously Helen was not going to give up on Phillip, she surmised. But then she saw Helen looking in Herbert's direction and wondered if perhaps she might be interested in him instead.

Those two would make a perfect couple. Not only did both of their names begin with the letter "H," but they also had a multitude of traits in common, none of which Teddi admired. However, she decided that they probably deserved each other.

Before the service officially began, Phillip stood up and announced that a young adults' Bible study would begin on Wednesday nights after the first of the year. Enthusiastically extending an invitation to all those young people, he then asked them to spread the word among their friends in Junction City and Fort Riley. Once the announcements were completed, Sergeant Little went forward to lead the singing. His rich baritone voice boomed through the small chapel, encouraging those in attendance to join him in praising the Lord.

When the singing had ended, Phillip walked to the podium and began his sermon. He spoke about deceit and broken relationships among humans, comparing those to man breaking his relationship with God. His words were eloquent, but as Teddi listened to the words, she wondered if the sermon was aimed at her and the occurrences of the previous night. Surely he couldn't have written and delivered so powerful a sermon with only a few hours of preparation. Or could he? If the sermon dealt with personal events and feelings, he may not have needed much time at all. Her mind was racing by the time the service ended, and when they finally reached the back of the church, she noticed Phillip looking her way as he was shaking hands with one of the soldiers.

"I'm not going to make it for dinner today. There's something I must attend to immediately," he hurriedly explained.

Teddi noticed him looking at someone behind her as he spoke, but didn't turn to look. It might be Herbert, and she didn't want a scene before she spoke privately with Phillip.

"I truly need to talk to you, Phillip. Isn't it something that could wait just a couple of hours?" she asked. She didn't want to keep him from his pastoral duties, although she couldn't keep the sound of urgency out of her voice.

"Are you ill? Your color doesn't look good," he said while taking her hand.

"I didn't get much sleep last night. Were you at the ball? I never did see you," she continued as the line formed behind her.

"Yes, I was there. If I don't have time to stop by your

house today, we can talk at work tomorrow," he said, nodding toward the crowd that was gathering to shake his hand.

"Yes, of course," she quietly replied.

What else could she do but agree? It was obvious he wasn't going to change his mind. Turning to leave, Teddi permitted herself a quick look over her shoulder. Helen Hanson stood directly in Phillip's line of vision, her hand raised to cover her mouth as she whispered something to Mattie. Teddi watched the twosome as she stood waiting for her parents in the vestibule of the church. Their whispering was continual, as was Helen's obvious admiration of Phillip. Her stare remained fixed on him until Teddi and her parents left the church.

"I'd be pleased to take Phillip's place at your dinner table," Herbert said when General Yorke had gone to fetch the sleigh.

Isabelle turned on her heel and pointed her finger in Herbert's face. "You are not welcome at our dinner table or in our house. Leave Teddi alone, or you'll have my husband and sons to contend with, Herbert, and I know you don't want that. Since you've already shown what you're made of, I'm sure you'll want to avoid a confrontation with the Yorke men!"

Herbert merely nodded and gave them an evil grin. "Remember, Teddi, things aren't always what they seem. I'm going to look very appealing to you in a short time."

"What does he mean by that?" Isabelle asked as Clayton arrived with the sleigh.

"I don't know, Mother. He's said several strange things about the future."

"Was that Albright I saw?" Clayton asked as he assisted the women.

"Yes, Father, but I hope Mother has made it abundantly clear he should stay away."

They rode home in silence, except for the sound of the jingling sleigh bells. But even the bells didn't improve Teddi's mood. What was so important that Phillip couldn't spare her a few hours? Helen Hanson? She *was* standing there and waiting after church.

Her brothers and their dates came alongside them in another sleigh and immediately challenged Clayton to a race.

"To the Republican River Bridge and back. How does that sound?" Clayton called out.

"Sounds good," Jonathan yelled as he slapped the reins and moved ahead before Clayton could say anything further.

"Turn this sleigh around, Clayton. I need to get home. We're having guests for dinner," Isabelle ordered.

"Your guests are all in that sleigh we're racing, Isabelle, so sit back and enjoy the ride," Clayton replied with a boisterous laugh, obviously delighted with the competition.

Teddi was as disgruntled as her mother with the light-hearted race that her brothers and their girlfriends seemed to be enjoying. She wanted to go home and spend time in her room thinking, and perhaps talk to her brothers and see if they had heard anything or could help solve this riddle. But they were too busy enjoying themselves to be concerned about her problems, she decided.

By the time they reached the bridge, Clayton had gained and the horses were neck and neck as they began their turn. Clayton brought his team around, keeping them in a tighter turn, and when they were back on the straightaway, he was in the lead. Teddi pulled the buffalo robe up around her mother and noticed a familiar sleigh coming toward them, headed toward Junction City. The sun was shining brightly, causing a blinding glare as it hit the whiteness of the snow. Cupping her palm above her eyes, she stared off in the direction of the sleigh. She was right; it was Phillip. Phillip, Helen Hanson, Mattie, and *Herbert?* She turned around and stared after them, unable to believe her eyes. However, just when she was sure it couldn't possibly be true, Herbert stood up in the back of the sleigh and waved.

What was going on? What reason would Phillip have to be in the company of those three people? And why would he want to be with them rather than her? He had said there was something he had to attend to, but what business could he possibly have with them?

"Was that Phillip?" her mother asked, a look of astonishment crossing her face.

Teddi nodded her head, but remained silent. Her stomach began to roll, and she felt bile rising in the back of her throat.

"It looked like Helen and Herbert in the sleigh with him," Isabelle continued without noticing that Teddi had grown unusually quiet. "That couldn't be, could it?" she asked, now looking at her daughter.

"You really are ill. I should have permitted you to stay home from church this morning. Hurry up, Clayton. We need to get Teddi home," Isabelle shouted to her husband.

"In case you hadn't noticed, I'm in a race, Isabelle. These horses won't go any faster, or they'd already be doing it," he hollered back over his shoulder.

"Well, find the quickest route home," she commanded, unwilling to allow him the final word. "Not much longer, dear," she said to Teddi in a soothing voice. "We're almost back to the fort."

Within a few minutes, Clayton pulled the team to a halt and jumped down to help Teddi out of the sleigh. "Let me help you upstairs," he said, placing his arm around her waist as they walked into the house and up the stairs.

Isabelle stopped in the kitchen to issue a few orders to Florence; then she secured a pitcher of fresh water and a cloth. That accomplished, she scurried up the steps, nearly spilling the water on Clayton as he was leaving the bedroom.

"Let's get you out of that dress," Isabelle said as she entered the room.

"I can't move right now, Mother. I'll take off my dress as

soon as I feel a little better," Teddi groaned. "Go take care of your guests. I'll be fine."

"I'm going to have Jonathan bring up a bell so that you can ring if you want me. There's a fresh pitcher of water right here if you need it. When you're ready to get out of your dress or if you want something to eat, just ring the bell."

"Fine, Mother, but I really don't think I'll need you."

Arguing would serve no purpose. If her mother decided a bell was needed, there would be a bell in the room! Teddi rolled over and watched the door. No matter how awful she felt, she wanted to speak to Jonathan. Moments later her brother appeared at the door dangling a bell between his index finger and thumb.

"You rang?" he asked while jingling the bell. "How are you feeling?"

"I'll be all right. I think it's more a lack of sleep and a series of unsettling circumstances that have me upset. Have you talked to Phillip?"

Jonathan shook his head. "Just for a minute at church, but he seemed preoccupied with the crowd, so I said we'd see him for dinner later. That's all. I didn't see him at the party last night. You did find him, didn't you?"

"No. I thought he was the Irishman, but it turned out to be Herbert. It's a long story, and I'm sure Mother will share all the gruesome details at dinner. When I'm feeling better, I'd like to talk with you."

"Just let me know when you're ready. Now get some rest, and maybe you'll feel strong enough to come down later and join us," he instructed as he left the room.

The sounds of laughter and clanging china floated up the stairway as Teddi relaxed and fell into a deep sleep.

thirteen

Phillip squinted his eyes against the brilliance of the sun glistening on the expanse of chalky-white snow that stretched before him. He could feel his heartbeat increasing as blood pulsed through his veins. His head was pounding. Taking both reins in his left hand, he massaged his right temple, then switched hands and began rubbing the left side of his head. It was at that moment that he noticed two sleighs racing toward him, and one of them was strikingly familiar.

Straining, he kept his gaze fixed upon the sleigh on the left. Surely it couldn't be. But as the two teams raced alongside each other, he knew his eyesight hadn't betrayed him; it was the Yorkes, and Teddi was looking in his direction. He turned his head, hoping she wouldn't recognize the sleigh—or him, for that matter. But he knew it was unlikely that they would go unnoticed, especially when he turned and saw Herbert standing up and wildly waving his arms at Teddi.

"Sit down before I knock you down," Phillip shouted over his shoulder.

"Just wanted to be sure Teddi saw that you were in such fine company," Herbert shouted back.

His words and the evil laugh that followed reinforced what Phillip already knew. This whole group was up to no good, and he was going to find himself smack in the middle of their depravity. He had fallen prey to Helen's conniving plot at every turn, from following her outdoors the previous night, to having Herbert Albright in his sleigh at this very moment.

Mattie seemed somewhat distressed with the situation, but Phillip realized that Mattie would do whatever Helen ordered.

The poor girl was obviously afraid of losing the only friend she had, but too shallow to realize that Helen didn't even know the true meaning of friendship. He didn't know if there was any way Mattie could help, but even if she could, he doubted his ability to win her allegiance.

"Where are we going?" Phillip finally asked when they had arrived in Junction City.

"Mattie's house. There's nobody home, and we can talk privately," Herbert replied, pointing for Phillip to turn east on First Street and then motioning him to turn in beside a small frame house.

Helen and Mattie jumped down from the sleigh as Phillip tied the horses and followed Herbert onto the front porch of the modest home.

"My parents will be home by five o'clock. You've got to be out of here by then," Mattie warned as she opened the front door and permitted them entry.

"This won't take long. I'm sure Phillip is going to be *very* cooperative," Herbert sneered, leading them into the parlor.

Herbert and both of the girls removed their coats, but Phillip remained encased in his heavy, wool greatcoat, removing only his gloves and hat.

"Sit down, sit down, my good man. We're not going to torture you, merely have a civil little chat," Herbert said in a cunning voice.

Phillip obeyed the command by perching himself on the edge of a padded wicker chair, certain that he wanted to take flight and even more certain that nothing good was going to come from this meeting. Absently twirling a lock of hair around her finger, Helen was poised on the sofa with Herbert flanking her on one side and Mattie on the other. All three of them turned and focused their attention upon him.

"It seems you've caused a bit of a problem in my life, and, fortunately for all of us, I've found a reasonable solution. I think it will make all of us happy, perhaps with the exception of you, Phillip. But since you're a man of God, I'm sure you'll learn to adjust, and in time you may even be thankful for what is going to occur. And when that time comes, please remember that you have me to thank for your good fortune, not God," Herbert said.

"There's no need to blaspheme," Mattie whispered.

"Poor, dear Mattie. She's afraid God is going to strike her dead for her part in this little charade. I can't seem to convince her otherwise. Why don't you give her your assurance that she's not going to burn in hell for merely corroborating Helen's statements?" Herbert said, his tone condescending.

"Mattie knows the real truth and also knows how to avoid burning in hell, don't you, Mattie?" Phillip asked.

Mattie nodded her head. "Reverend Lewis says you have to accept Jesus into your heart as your very own personal Savior and repent of all your sins, and if you do that, you'll go to heaven," Mattie replied.

"And have you done that, Mattie?" Phillip asked in a kind voice.

"Oh, shut up," Herbert angrily interrupted. "This isn't some tent revival, and you're not going to save her soul while I have more important things to take care of. You have something that I want, *and* you have something that our sweet, little Helen wants. Now, this can be a very simple thing if you'll cooperate, or it can be very ugly if you don't."

"How could I possibly have anything that either one of you wants?" Phillip asked.

"If you'll let me finish, I'll tell you. Unfortunately, my poor wife of only a few months met with an untimely death, leaving me once again a single man. Since your arrival at Fort Riley, you've been pursuing the woman I intend to marry."

"What kind of a man are you? You've just buried your wife, and now you come here telling me you intend to marry Teddi

Yorke. Well, sir, she'll never have you!" Phillip exclaimed.

"There you go, interrupting again. I have this all worked out, Phillip, and if you'll just listen, you'll soon see that she *will* have me. In fact, I dare say she'll be thrilled that *anyone* would consider marrying her after the humiliation you've caused her."

Helen looked at Herbert as though he were a genius ready to solve all the mysteries of life, while poor Mattie nervously fidgeted about, jumping up and down to peek out the heavily layered, emerald green draperies and then returning to her appointed position beside Helen on the settee.

"What are you talking about? I've done nothing to cause her shame or embarrassment," Phillip defended.

"Do you hear that, Helen?" Herbert asked, giving Helen a look of amazement. "Why, he's already forgotten what he did to you last night. The scoundrel!" Herbert sarcastically exclaimed.

"Phillip, don't you remember last night in your sleigh? Although I protested violently, you took advantage of me—a poor, defenseless, young woman. You've stolen that which is most prized among all unmarried women. What man would want me now that I've been defiled? You have an obligation to marry me!"

"That's a lie, and you know it. I never laid a hand on you, although you used your wiles to try to entice me to do so. I'll deny it. Nobody will believe such a story."

"Won't they? Mattie, get back over here and tell Reverend Hamilton what you saw," Herbert commanded.

Mattie once again moved away from the window and back to the sofa. Sitting down beside Helen, she lowered her eyes and spoke. "I came outside looking for Helen when the two of you had been gone from the party for such a long time. When I got close to your sleigh, I heard Helen crying, saying that you had ruined her and begging you to marry her since you had stolen her virtue."

"You heard *what?* And what did *I* say, Mattie?" Phillip asked.

"You? Oh, you said that you couldn't marry her even though you truly wanted to, because she's the most beautiful woman in the world."

After she had spoken the words, Mattie stopped for a moment and looked at Helen, her eyes seeming to seek out the other woman's approval.

"Go on, Mattie. You're doing a wonderful job. Tell him the rest," Helen encouraged.

Mattie nodded her head and gave Helen a smile. "You said you found Teddi Yorke completely undesirable, but you were going to marry her because you knew her father had inherited a lot of money, and one day you'd get your share of it. Then you said that marrying Teddi would probably help your military career, too, and that Helen had nothing but her beauty to offer. And then," Mattie continued dramatically, "you said that you would keep Helen as your *mistress.*"

The last words were barely audible, and Phillip strained to hear her declaration. He could feel the blood rush to his face as he jumped up from his chair, his anger barely under control as he moved in front of the trio of conspirators.

"How dare you! Who do you think is going to give credence to this host of lies? I can't believe that the three of you have collaborated to manipulate and ruin the reputations and lives of others in such a callous, unfeeling manner. What is wrong with you? Are you all so insecure and pitiful that you can't build a relationship with another person except by deceit and lies? You're a pathetic group of human beings."

Only Mattie looked uncomfortable with the words he'd spoken. Helen and Herbert merely glanced at each other, as if they had expected such a reaction and were quite willing to take it in stride.

"I will not be a party to any of this. I won't marry you, Helen. I won't permit you to seduce Teddi under the pretense of lies, Herbert. And I won't allow you to denigrate my name with your lies, Mattie. Now if that's all you have to say, I'm leaving," Phillip proclaimed.

"You may want to give this a little thought. A court-martial could be an ugly smear on your good name. I'm sure Teddi Yorke wouldn't consider marrying someone who left the military with less than an honorable discharge. And then there's your reputation, *Reverend*. Whatever are your parishioners going to think of a preacher who would ruthlessly frolic about underneath the blankets of his sleigh while a party was going on only a short distance away? I don't think they'd be very pleased. Shame, shame," Herbert replied, shaking his finger at Phillip and giving him a depraved laugh.

"People will believe me," Phillip avowed.

"Perhaps if it were only your word against sweet, little Helen's. But with Mattie to take an oath and swear the story is gospel—well, I don't think you have much of a chance. As I said, give it some thought. I'll come by the hospital tomorrow afternoon, say about four-thirty. Or would you prefer that I come to the church instead, since the object of our affections may be at the hospital?" he asked, a smirk twisting the corners of his mouth.

"I'm not concerned about Teddi seeing you. I'll be at the hospital at four-thirty, just as I am every weekday. Suit yourself as to whether you come or not," Phillip replied as he pulled on his gloves and donned his black beaver hat.

Mattie was standing guard at the front door as Phillip entered the small foyer. "I'm sorry, Reverend Hamilton. But Helen's my friend, and she needs my help," the girl whispered.

"And do you think that makes what you're doing right in the eyes of God, Mattie?" Phillip whispered back.

"No," she replied, shaking her head back and forth, her

lower lip trembling. "But perhaps someday God will forgive me my sin. Helen would *never* forgive me if I betrayed her."

"Did you listen to my sermon today, Mattie? About how we humans break our relationship with God?" he asked, still keeping his voice low.

The girl nodded her head up and down. "I know, but—"

"What are you two whispering about out there?" Herbert hollered, jumping up from the settee and coming toward them.

"Nothing you'd be interested in, I'm sure," Phillip replied as he pulled open the door and hastened down the steps toward his sleigh.

ঽৡ

A loud rapping on the front door awakened Teddi from a restless sleep. She could hear Ruth Ann's laughter and then Jonathan's voice as he opened the front door and shouted a greeting to Phillip. Jumping up from the bed, Teddi rushed to the bureau, grabbed her comb, and began to straighten her disheveled hair with one hand while using the other to straighten the wrinkles from her rumpled dress.

She heard Jonathan racing up the steps, taking them two at a time until he reached the hallway. "You awake, Teddi? Phillip is downstairs wanting to talk to you."

"Yes. Tell him I'll be down in a moment," she replied, glancing in the mirror and pinching each of her cheeks, which she hoped would add a tint to her colorless complexion. Pressing her fingers down the front of her dress one last time, she decided there was nothing more that could be done to straighten the dress without the aid of a flatiron, and made her way downstairs.

Phillip rushed to the bottom of the staircase as soon as she turned at the landing and stepped onto the lower flight of stairs. At least he was anxious to see her. Perhaps that was a good sign.

"We need to talk," Phillip said in a hushed tone. "Is there

somewhere we can speak privately?"

Teddi glanced toward the parlor where her parents, brothers, Ruth Ann, and Margaret were engaged in conversation. "I suppose we could go out to the kitchen. I don't think Florence will be in there right now."

He nodded his head and followed behind, seating himself opposite her on a wooden stool. His face was etched with concern, and perhaps a bit of anger. He must have heard the rumors about her agreeing to marry Herbert, Teddi decided.

When he opened his mouth to speak, she immediately interrupted him. "Phillip, let me say my piece; then I'll listen to whatever it is you want to tell me," she pleaded. "There is no way I could give my full attention to what you're about to say unless you've heard me out beforehand."

He seemed confused by her statement but didn't argue, and for that she was grateful. It would take all the courage she could muster to speak of last night's events, and if he argued with her, she knew that she would lose her boldness.

"I saw you in the sleigh with Herbert and Helen, and I'm sure that Herbert has already told you what occurred last night," she began. He visibly winced at her words, but he didn't speak, so she continued. "It is true that I agreed to marry Herbert," she said, watching the disbelief that crossed his face at her pronouncement.

"What? You say you agreed to marry that immoral rogue? I don't believe it!" he exclaimed, leaping up from the stool and causing it to hurl backward to the floor in a riotous crash.

"Didn't he tell you?" she asked, stunned by his seeming lack of knowledge.

"No, he *didn't* give me that bit of information. "If you've agreed to marry him, then why is he coercing me?"

"I agreed only because I thought it was you," she whispered. "He was dressed in costume and used an Irish accent. I truly believed it was you. He took me back into one of the dressing rooms. It was dark, and he kissed me and asked that I pledge my love and promise to marry him. I'm sorry, Phillip. I've embarrassed myself *and* you. After he revealed his identity, I told him I would *never* consider marriage. But my refusal didn't stop him from going about the room telling the other guests that I had agreed to marry him. Can you ever forgive me?" she asked, gasping to take a breath.

"There is nothing for me to forgive. You're blameless. But when I've finished my tale, you may feel otherwise," he said.

She sat with her back straight and a stoic expression on her face as Phillip then recounted how he had taken the woman, whom he soon discovered was actually Helen, out to his sleigh. He related how Helen had used the same trickery as Herbert, luring him to the sleigh by pretending to be Teddi—how she'd worn a costume that padded her figure and had effected a Southern drawl.

Teddi wasn't sure she cared to hear the details of Helen being required to pad her figure in order to pass herself off as Teddi. But, no matter how hard it might have been to hear, she knew that padding would have been a necessary part of Helen's clever costume. By the time Phillip had completed the details of his trip into Junction City, Teddi was aghast at the malicious scheme Herbert and Helen had devised.

"Now, I must ask if you can forgive me and believe that what I have told you is true?" Phillip somberly inquired.

She nodded her agreement, and, after a brief conversation with her father, Teddi returned to the kitchen. Moments later she heard Ruth Ann and Margaret bidding her parents farewell and the sound of sleigh bells jingling as her brothers hitched the team and drove the sleigh around to the front of the house.

fourteen

Phillip spent a restless night and rose the next morning feeling as though he'd never gone to bed. It would be a long day, and the four thirty appointment with Herbert loomed over him like a thundercloud on a spring day. Teddi arrived at her appointed time and appeared well rested, greeting him with a cheery "good morning" as she waved and headed off toward the ward to care for the patients.

He was astounded. She hadn't even stopped to tell him what had happened after he had left their quarters last night. When Jonathan and George hadn't returned by nine o'clock, the general had instructed his wife to leave a note for them to waken him when they got home; then he announced that he was off to bed and suggested that Phillip do the same.

Teddi had shrugged her shoulders at his questioning glance and advised him that if her father suggested that he go home and get some rest, he'd best do so. She had bid him good night, seeming assured that their problem was under control. Unfortunately, Phillip didn't share her optimism. After returning home, he had spent several hours on his knees seeking God's direction, and, although he hadn't received an answer, he had experienced a bit of pain in his knees when he attempted to stand up and get into bed.

And now, without any form of explanation, Teddi had just marched into the hospital and had left him totally in the dark. Phillip now found himself in a quandary. What if Clayton, George, and Jonathan had never met to devise a plan to thwart Herbert? What if Herbert showed up at four thirty and Phillip had absolutely no plan of action? If the three Yorke men hadn't gotten together, perhaps Phillip could meet with them now. He needed answers, and he needed them soon! Rising from his chair, he purposefully marched off toward the hospital ward.

"We need to talk," Phillip whispered to Teddi as she stood near a patient's bed, checking his bandage.

"I'll be through here in about an hour. I can stop by your office then," she said, giving him a smile.

"No, you don't understand. We need to talk *now*," he said, his teeth gritted together and his blood pressure steadily increasing as they spoke.

She nodded. "Everything is fine, Phillip. I'll come to your office shortly," she said, continuing to wrap the soldier's bandage.

There was no need to continue the conversation. He could hardly argue with her in front of a ward filled with sick soldiers. Not knowing what else to do, he breathed a deep sigh, turned on his heel, and stalked off to his office.

During the next hour, he pulled his pocket watch out of his trousers at least every fifteen minutes, rose from his desk, paced to the doorway, and peered down the long, narrow hallway. Teddi was never there. After an hour had passed, his concern turned to fear; his fear turned to concern; and his concern finally turned to anger. Why didn't she come and talk to him? Was this some sort of torture? Just when he had determined to drag her back to his office if she wouldn't voluntarily return, the front door of the hospital opened. Phillip felt himself relax when Clayton, Jonathan, and George entered the building.

"I'm certainly glad to see the three of you. I can't get your daughter to talk to me," he said, looking at Clayton.

"I told her we'd be coming by to explain things. There were a few details we needed to work out. No need to have Teddi give you a plan of action that we might be required to change. Simpler that way," he said, obviously unconcerned about the fact that Phillip was now at his wit's end.

"Well, it may have seemed that way, but I was about to go in and demand that Teddi speak with me. It may be difficult for you to imagine, General, but I'm a bit on edge," Phillip replied while attempting to keep his temper in check.

"Have a little faith, son—in God. . .and in me. I told you that I'd develop a plan. We're going to go over it, and when Albright arrives, you'll put it into action," he said, pulling up a chair. "Sit down, boys," he ordered as he leaned back, unbuttoned his coat, and began to lay out his strategy.

"So what do you think? Can you carry it off?" the general inquired once he'd finished.

Phillip nodded his head. "Sure, I should be able to do it. Now all we have to do is wait until four-thirty arrives. I'm afraid it's going to be a long afternoon."

Teddi entered Phillip's office a short time later, greeting the general and her brothers with enthusiasm. Although Teddi didn't win her debate with Clayton wherein she attempted to remain at the hospital, they all agreed that she had waged a laudable argument. Their praise didn't seem to appease her, but she did as she had been ordered, bidding Phillip good-bye at four o'clock, after he promised to come to their quarters immediately after Herbert left.

Herbert arrived at the appointed time, neither a minute early nor a minute late. He walked into the hospital as if he owned the place, his pompous attitude causing Phillip to bridle. However, he knew he *had* to control himself. Anger would not serve him well if their plan was to go as intended. Steeling himself, he held out his hand to Herbert, giving him a gratuitous smile, all the while wishing he could ball his hand into a fist and shove it down the deadbeat's throat.

"Well, here we are," Herbert said as he pulled off his overcoat and threw it onto one of the chairs. "I assume I'm welcome to have a seat?" he acerbically questioned.

"Sit, stand—it makes no difference to me. You're the one who arranged this meeting," Phillip replied tersely.

"Well, at least it should be a short meeting. What's your answer?"

"Before I give you my answer, I want to be sure that I completely understand the ground rules," Phillip replied, easing himself back in his chair.

"Oh, I think you understand," Herbert replied.

"This is a lifelong commitment you're forcing upon me. I think I'm entitled to be sure I have a thorough understanding of the facts," Phillip countered.

"What is it you want to review?" Herbert asked, clearly annoyed.

"As I understand it, you and Helen have both decided that rather than Teddi and I exploring the possibility of marriage to each other, you intend to marry Teddi in the hope of achieving higher military rank and possibly gaining a sizable inheritance. Helen, on the other hand, has declared that she will lie under oath in order to have me court-martialed, claiming that I took advantage of her the night of the masquerade ball. Unless, of course, I agree to marry her. In that case, she will suddenly forget all of those alleged facts, and we will enter into wedded bliss," Phillip recounted.

"That's about it. Of course, you've left out a few minor points, such as the fact that Mattie is willing to corroborate Helen's testimony. Oh, I think I may have forgotten to mention that Teddi *has* agreed to marry me. Naturally, I was sure to spread that information last Saturday night—promoting public acceptance in advance, you might say," Herbert stated smugly.

"And now you expect me to roll over and accept this deceitful contrivance?"

"I think doing so probably outweighs the alternatives," Herbert chuckled.

"Well, I don't!" General Yorke announced, walking

through an adjacent doorway with Jonathan and George following close behind.

"What are—what are *they* doing here?" Herbert stammered.

"We're listening to your lies so that *we* may act as Phillip's corroborating witnesses at the court-martial you and your accomplices are proposing. This whole situation is repugnant. If anyone is court-martialed, it won't be Phillip. It will be *you*," the general snarled.

With only a moment to regain his composure, Herbert was once again on the offensive. "Ah, but General, don't you think that when I bring to the board's attention the fact that you and your sons are merely seeking to protect your daughter's interests, the board members may look upon your testimony with a jaundiced eye? The fact that you are the commander of this military reservation may cause the board to scrutinize your testimony very closely. After all, the military and civilians, as well as the press, would be quick to point out the fact that you might unduly influence the members sitting on the court-martial board. In fact, I think your testimony could very well work in our favor."

"Don't you count on that," General Yorke replied, his face turning bright red.

"I'm not concerned that you've overheard this conversation, gentlemen—not in the least," Herbert replied as he picked up his coat. "Since I've given you additional food for thought, Phillip, I'll give you a little longer to come to a final decision. I will expect your answer by Wednesday—right after the church service would be a good time, don't you think? It will give you that final opportunity to pray for a miracle," he snickered as he gave the general an irreverent salute and confidently strode out of the room.

"He's not the least bit concerned. And, unfortunately, he did make a valid point. The court-martial board would weigh your testimony against your connection to Teddi and me,"

Phillip remarked.

"We need to think this through. It's almost time for supper, and crisis or not, my stomach is growling to be fed. Let's get home and have some dinner. We'll think better once we've eaten. At least *I* will," Clayton exclaimed.

"Come along, my friend. I'm sure Teddi is champing at the bit to hear what's happened," Jonathan said as he pulled Phillip a few steps ahead of his father and George. "We'll get the sleigh. The two of you can wait here and keep warm."

The general nodded his acceptance of the offer, and George was more than willing to wait with his father in the warmth of the hospital while the two other men trudged off to retrieve the sleigh. They had descended the final porch step, when Jonathan threw his arm across Phillip's shoulder.

"Would you like to hear some good news in the midst of all this turmoil that's swirling about?" Jonathan asked as they rounded the corner of the building.

"Certainly," Phillip halfheartedly replied.

"That didn't sound very enthusiastic!"

"Sorry, but it's a little difficult for me to get excited about much of anything right now," Phillip said.

"I understand, but keep your faith, Phillip. I agree with my father—this will work out. Now for my news: I've asked Margaret to marry me—and she's accepted!"

"You hardly know Margaret! Don't you think this is a little sudden, Jonathan? Besides, you'll be leaving in a couple of weeks, and then what?"

"How long does it take to fall in love when you meet the right woman? Aren't *you* the one who was telling me you were going to settle down as soon as you found a good woman?"

"Yes, but what about your family? Do they know? Do you think they'll be pleased with your choice? Don't misunderstand what I'm saying, Jonathan; I think Margaret is a lovely, young lady and a good woman. However, it can make for a rocky beginning to your life together if your families aren't in agreement," Phillip cautioned.

"I'm well beyond the age of needing my parents' approval, although I would prefer that all parties be in agreement. Margaret said she was certain her parents wouldn't have any objection. I think my mother is the only one who may disapprove. Unlike my father, she tends to worry about gossip. However, Teddi tells me that she and Mother have had several conversations lately concerning the topic of genuine forgiveness, and Mother's attitude has changed a great deal."

"Teddi's wisdom never ceases to amaze me!"

"Our Teddi may not be a raving beauty, but she's a very special woman, and that's a fact," Jonathan concluded as he drove the sleigh toward the front of the hospital.

"Well, whatever you and Margaret decide, I'm rooting for you. Just remember that I expect to be the one presiding over your vows," Phillip said while giving Jonathan a slap on the back.

"The cold air seems to have enlivened your spirits," the general said as he approached the sleigh. "It always does the same for me. Nothing better than cold weather and an invigorating snowfall."

Phillip attempted to give Teddi an encouraging smile as he entered the house, encircled by her father and brothers. She was searching his face, obviously looking for a clue, but he followed the general's advice and waited until after dinner. Isabelle and Florence were nowhere in sight, but the mouthwatering smells that permeated the house sent all four of the men searching after food. They had the scent and were like dogs to the hunt, unwilling to stop until they located their quarry.

Isabelle appeared from the kitchen, an apron tied around her waist and her cheeks flushed from the oven's heat. She carried loaves of freshly baked, crusty bread and placed them on cutting boards at either end of the table. A sharp knife and small crock of churned butter sat beside each loaf. A large tureen of beef stew was centered on the table.

"I thought we'd have a simple meal this evening. Thinking we may have some private matters to discuss, I told Florence she could have the evening to herself," Isabelle explained as she removed her apron before seating herself.

"That was an excellent idea, my dear. But if it's all the same to you, I'd rather wait to talk until after dinner," Clayton replied.

"After dinner Teddi and I will be busy serving coffee and clearing the table. Since we're the only ones who don't know what happened this afternoon, I'd prefer that we talk during dinner—if it won't upset your digestion," Isabelle added with a grin.

"There's not much that upsets my appetite or my digestion, but I'm hungry and would rather eat than talk. However, you're right. It's not fair to keep you two in the dark. I'll eat and you can tell them about this afternoon's happenings, Phillip," he said with one of his boisterous laughs.

Her father's upbeat conversation and jovial laughter seemed to relax Teddi, and Phillip now worried that she would consider the general's buoyant spirits a signal that things had gone well. Both women turned their gaze upon Phillip, but their looks of expectation were more than he cared to deal with at the moment. The general had cleverly sidestepped discussing the issue himself, and Phillip couldn't blame him. It was, after all, his own foolishness that had caused this predicament, and thus far, his prayers for a quick, quiet resolution to the situation had gone unanswered.

General Yorke was well into his second bowl of stew by the time Phillip had finished divulging the brutal details of the meeting with Herbert. His words had managed to erase any visible trace of joy from Teddi's demeanor, her face now etched with concern and dismay. His attempts to keep the mood lighthearted had fallen flat, and Teddi now looked at him as though he had utterly and completely failed her.

"I know it's of little consequence since the damage is already done, but how has Herbert managed to be so long absent from his military assignment, Clayton?" Isabelle asked, breaking the silence that had hung in the room.

"My guess would be that his commanding officer allowed him to come back to Junction City to spend time with his deceased wife's family—advise them of her death. I doubt his company would be leaving on a campaign until spring, so it's probable that he was given leave. I don't think he's a deserter, since one of his reasons for marrying Teddi is to help advance his military career."

Isabelle nodded her head, gave Teddi an encouraging smile, and began clearing the table. "I'll bring coffee to the parlor when you're ready," she said as the men began moving away from the table.

"Let the dishes go, Isabelle. I want you and Teddi to join us. We need all the help we can get if we're going to devise a plan that will set things aright," the general stated.

They talked, they prayed, and then they talked some more until finally the general announced it was time they get to bed. His decision was met with unanimous approval, although none of them was sure that anything had been solved, or for that matter, that anyone had even come up with one good idea.

≥≈

When Teddi didn't arrive at the hospital the next morning, Phillip was certain she had washed her hands of him, most likely deciding that the only way to make a clean break was to quit working with him. And why should he blame her? She would once again be subjected to ridicule, her name spilling off the wagging tongues of local gossips. It saddened him to realize how foolhardy and reckless he had been. When all was said and done, he'd be lucky if there would be any church that would have him, and his military career would certainly be in ruins. Perhaps, if he were lucky, he would be able to skulk away and practice medicine in some small community needing a doctor. It was a foregone conclusion that he could forget his plans for preaching the Word and winning souls for Christ. No church would desire a man who lacked the ability to keep himself free of such personal adversity.

It was sometime after one o'clock when he heard the door to the hospital open. He certainly could have used Teddi's assistance today. It seemed that every child living on the post had been dragged into the dispensary with varying complaints throughout the morning, and now it sounded as though it was going to continue through the afternoon hours.

"I'm sorry I didn't get word to you that I wouldn't make it in this morning," Teddi said as she greeted him in the hallway. "Have you been busy?"

Just seeing her caused his heart to lighten. "I'm so happy to see you," he exclaimed, a smile spreading across his face. "Let me take your coat," he offered as he rushed to assist her. "I *was* worried when you didn't arrive, thinking perhaps you'd decided it better to stay away from the likes of me."

"Do you think I have so little character that I would actually desert you, Phillip?" she asked in a pain-filled voice.

He took her hands in his own and met her intense gaze. He was certain her eyes were filled with as much love and concern as his own. Turning over each of her hands, he bent his head down and tenderly kissed the palms of her hands, his lips trailing up each hand until he reached her fingertips.

"I am so very sorry," he murmured, his head still bowed. "Can you ever forgive me for being such a fool?"

"Is your memory so short that you don't remember I've already forgiven you, Phillip?"

"You forgave me, but that was before we knew all of this

was going to turn into a public spectacle. The court-martial will turn into a feeding frenzy for the gossips, and I know how much you detest being at the center of such idle chatter."

"My forgiveness wasn't conditional. If there's one lesson that God has recently taught me, it's forgiveness. I don't want to make the same mistake with others that I made with Margaret. Public humiliation is a small price to pay for doing what is just, and only God knows what will eventually happen. We both know that He is at work in every situation, and I feel an assurance that no matter how all of this turns out, we're going to be fine," she said.

"I should be ashamed of myself. I'm a preacher, supposedly a man of God, yet I need you to keep me grounded in my faith. You are, in every way, the woman I have prayed I would find. Now I pray that I won't lose you," he whispered.

"Oh, Phillip, you won't lose me. We're going to stand our ground, declare the truth, and rely upon the hand of God to see us through," she replied confidently.

fifteen

Teddi sat beside her brother on the settee while Isabelle perched on the edge of her rocking chair, staring at them in disbelief. No one spoke for several minutes, and the crackling fire was the only sound that broke the deafening silence that hung in the room.

"You need to give this more time, Jonathan. We'll discuss it with your father and get his opinion," Isabelle asserted, her chin jutting forward as she spoke.

"I didn't tell you in order to secure your permission or your opinion, Mother, although I would be pleased to have your blessing. However, whether you and Father agree has nothing to do with my decision. I plan to marry Margaret. You and Father may be as involved in, or detached from, the process as you wish."

"Oh, good, here's your father now," Isabelle stated, projecting herself from the edge of the rocker and rushing toward Clayton. "I'm so glad you've come home. We have another crisis."

"I don't have time for another crisis, Isabelle. I merely came home to gather some papers and a map I need at my office. I'm sure you can capably handle any household crisis that has arisen with more expertise than I could muster," Clayton replied.

"This *isn't* a household matter. Jonathan is getting married," she announced without further fanfare.

"Well, that's good news. I was beginning to think you would never take a wife," Clayton stated as he walked into the parlor and embraced Jonathan. "So what's the crisis,

Isabelle? You can't find a new dress in time?" Clayton asked, emitting a loud guffaw.

"Oh, stop it, Clayton—this isn't funny. And before you go any further with your congratulations, I think you need to know who it is your son is planning to marry," Isabelle chastised.

"If I were a betting man, which I'm not, I'd put my money on Margaret," Clayton said. "Am I right?"

"Yes, you're right," Jonathan replied.

"Well, congratulations to you. I doubt that you could do better. She's bright, pretty, and devout in her Christian beliefs. Couldn't ask for much more than that. Can she cook?" Clayton asked, once again laughing at his own question.

Isabelle dropped into her rocker with a thud. "Is that *all* you have to say?" she asked.

"What else is there to say?" Clayton asked as he gathered up papers from the dining room. He waved his paperwork in the air as he hastened toward the front door, leaving as quickly as he'd entered. Jonathan had settled back onto the settee beside Teddi, while Isabelle vigorously rocked in her chair. Except for a faint squeak from one of the rockers on Isabelle's chair, silence reigned.

Finally Isabelle ceased her rocking and rose from the chair. "I'd like to talk to Margaret. Go into town and fetch her. She can eat lunch with us, and then we'll talk—alone," Isabelle instructed her son.

Jonathan didn't argue or comment. After donning his coat and gloves, he bid them good-bye, stating that he and Margaret would be back in time for lunch.

"See to preparations for lunch, Teddi. Florence can help you. I need to go upstairs," Isabelle commanded.

"Mother, Phillip is expecting me at the hospital. I'm already late," Teddi replied.

"This is more important. I'm sure that if there's an emergency, he'll send one of the soldiers over to advise you,"

Isabelle absently replied as she marched up the stairs.

ஃ

As if on cue, her mother descended the stairs at the exact moment Jonathan and Margaret entered the front door. Teddi watched as her mother greeted Margaret with a seemingly genuine hug and exchanged pleasantries about the weather and the approaching holiday festivities. Isabelle had changed her dress, and although her eyes seemed slightly red and puffy, she appeared in good spirits as she presided over lunch.

Jonathan appeared somewhat edgy when Florence was serving her warm bread pudding for dessert, and by the time the meal was finally completed, his complexion had paled, and he looked as though he would grab Margaret and bolt from the room. Margaret, however, seemed relaxed as she chatted about the new arrival of goods at her father's store, including some special items that he had received just in time to delight Christmas shoppers.

"Teddi, you'd better hurry on over to the hospital. Jonathan can take you in the sleigh. Do stay and visit with Phillip for a while, Jonathan. Margaret and I are going to have a little chat of our own," Isabelle stated.

"I think I'll remain here. You don't mind taking the sleigh by yourself, do you, Teddi?" Jonathan inquired.

Before Teddi had an opportunity to reply, Isabelle was rising from her chair. "Don't be difficult, Jonathan. It's an excellent opportunity for you to spend a little free time with your friend. Once you return to Washington, you don't know when you'll be back to Kansas. Oh, and ask Phillip if he'd like to join us for supper. You *will* stay for dinner, too, won't you?" Isabelle asked as she turned toward Margaret.

Margaret looked toward Jonathan, obviously unsure how she should answer. "You may plan on our being here for dinner," he began, "unless—"

"Good," Isabelle said, interrupting her son. "Now get

along to the hospital," she ordered, waving her arms at them as though she were shooing chickens out of the barnyard.

"If necessary, I think Margaret can hold her own with Mother," Teddi said as she and Jonathan left in the sleigh. "Not that she would ever be disrespectful, but Margaret is a strong woman who has a great deal of courage. Don't worry,"

"I don't feel quite so confident, but when Mother asked Margaret to stay for dinner, I took that as a good sign. Either that, or Mother has totally convinced herself that she can dissuade Margaret from accepting my proposal. Do you think that's possible?" Jonathan asked with a note of alarm in his voice.

Teddi giggled and threaded her arm through her brother's. "Oh, Jonathan, I don't think *anyone* could convince Margaret that you weren't created by God for the sole purpose of becoming her husband."

"I think that I would have to agree with that statement. Except, perhaps, that God may have had one or two other things for me to accomplish in addition to my marriage. But I won't tell Margaret that," he replied, giving his sister a broad smile. "Speaking of marriage, how are things with you and Phillip?" he asked with a grin.

"When I was late to work yesterday, he was convinced that I hadn't been able to forgive him and wouldn't be returning to work at the hospital. It took a bit of persuasion to convince him that my days of only paying lip service to forgiveness ended when God convicted me of my behavior toward Margaret. I think I've convinced him that my forgiveness wasn't based upon whether it would be easy or difficult to face the eventual consequences of his actions—or my own conduct, for that matter," she added. "I should never have left the party and gone off to the dressing room with Herbert, even if I *did* think he was Phillip. It wasn't appropriate behavior, and now I'll suffer the consequences. I'm sure

Herbert will leave no stone unturned in his attempts to prevail, but I wouldn't marry him if he were the last man left standing," Teddi vowed.

"Well, I hope that your late appearance today hasn't caused Phillip additional worry," Jonathan said as they arrived. "Let me help you out. Tell Phillip that I'll be in as soon as I've taken care of the horses. If he's busy, I'll just wait in his office."

Teddi nodded and rushed up the steps and into the hospital. After hanging her cloak in the vestibule, she peeked into Phillip's office, but when she noticed he was nowhere to be seen, she walked down the hallway and into the ward. Phillip was sitting beside the bed of a young soldier and was deep in conversation, so Teddi began checking charts and giving necessary medication to several of the men.

"I'm glad to see you," Phillip murmured as she stood by one of the soldiers who was suffering from a severe case of tonsillitis.

"Private Lowry seems to be responding to treatment and will be ready for discharge," Teddi commented.

"Private Lowry and I have agreed that perhaps he's enjoying the pleasure of extra rest and attention just a bit too much. We've agreed he'll be moving back to the barracks and assuming his regular duties tomorrow," Phillip advised with a slow, easy grin.

Teddi nodded her head. "That sounds like an excellent decision, gentlemen. By the way, my brother is in your office. He thought that the two of you might have a visit if you weren't too busy. I can finish up in here if you'd like to join him."

"Are you sure you don't mind?"

"Of course I don't. You two need to have some time to visit. Besides, I've been gone all morning, but Jonathan can explain that," she told him. "Oh, Mother invited you for dinner this evening if you're free," she added after he had turned to leave.

"I wouldn't miss it," he called back over his shoulder.

৶

Phillip made his way down the hall, trying to assume his usual jaunty step. He believed that Teddi had truly forgiven him, but the fact that he would be forced to meet with Herbert tomorrow after church loomed in his thoughts, a veritable thundercloud floating overhead, just waiting to deluge him.

"Jonathan, good to see you," Phillip cheerfully greeted him as he entered the office, his hand outstretched in welcome.

"Is that an act, or are you really feeling lighthearted?" Jonathan asked with a smile.

"You know me, my friend. I'm attempting to fight the good fight, but it hasn't been easy the past few days. It appears that Herbert isn't going to back down. I'll advise him that he and Helen can go ahead and file whatever charges they care to conjure up. Your father tells me we can push to have the board convene quickly. However, I'm concerned that you and George will be gone before the court-martial begins. And I'd guess that Herbert is counting on that fact. Barring a miracle, this may prove to be the darkest hour of my life. We'll all need to continue to pray that some good will come from all of this," Phillip replied.

"I wouldn't worry about the board not being able to convene before George and I leave. Father knows it's important for us to testify, and he knows when we'll be leaving the post. Personally, I hope it can take place before Christmas so that we can relax and enjoy the remainder of the holiday. And speaking of good coming from this incident, it appears my sister is quite smitten by your charms. And she tells me she wouldn't marry Herbert Albright if he were the last man left standing," Jonathan stated.

"Still, it's no way to begin a relationship."

"It can only make you stronger. Besides, it sounds to me as though this relationship has more than merely *just begun*," Jonathan gibed.

"I'd ask her to be my wife this very minute if it weren't for this pending difficulty," Phillip admitted. "And why aren't you visiting the lovely Margaret on this crisp December afternoon? I'm sure her company would be much more pleasant that my dour attitude."

"I would have to agree with that statement. However, Margaret is currently embroiled in conversation with my mother over at our quarters. I broke the news of our engagement to Mother early this morning. After quite a discussion, she ordered me to invite Margaret to lunch, stating that she intended to have a private talk with her. I went to town and told Margaret that I thought we should ignore Mother's command, but Margaret insisted, saying she didn't want to begin our marriage by showing disrespect toward either of my parents. Poor girl, she thinks that Mother will cave in and bless our union. Of course, Teddi seems to think Margaret can hold her own against Mother. We'll know by this evening. You *are* joining us for dinner, aren't you?"

Phillip nodded his head. "Teddi extended your mother's invitation. I'm not sure I'll be good company, but I always enjoy being with your family."

"Don't concern yourself with the need to be good company. I'm sure that hearing the outcome of my mother's conversation with Margaret will provide ample entertainment," Jonathan remarked.

Their afternoon of conversation was interrupted on several occasions by soldiers with varying ailments, along with a laundress who had severed her small finger while helping to butcher a hog. The bleeding had been intense, and Jonathan had fled the room in search of Teddi as soon as the woman entered Phillip's office. After Phillip and Teddi had managed to stop the bleeding and stitch the woman's hand, they turned her over to Jonathan, who agreed to take her home in the sleigh.

"We'll be ready to leave for home by the time you return," Teddi called after her brother as he helped the woman into the sleigh.

"Think he'll be all right?" Phillip asked with a grin.

"I'm not positive. He never could tolerate the sight of blood. I didn't think I was going to convince him that the sleigh ride wouldn't cause her to begin bleeding again. Sometimes it's hard to believe we're related," Teddi responded, returning his smile.

"Not so hard," Phillip said. "You are both genuinely kind-hearted people with a loving concern for your fellowman. Jonathan just has a little difficulty if his fellowman is bleeding."

It felt good to laugh. He hadn't laughed since all of this mess began at the masquerade ball. Somehow the holiday festivities had lost their luster. There had been no mention of the oyster dinner at the McCalebs' last night, and he was certain that none of the Yorkes had attended, although it was one of the most highly anticipated events of the year. Folks loved the oyster supper at the church, but the dinner at McCalebs' was an invitation-only affair that was served in their luxurious home, with no expense spared. Teddi had told him that once you were invited, it was something you didn't want to miss. But they had missed the anticipated affair without giving it as much as a single thought.

"Jonathan's here," Teddi announced, breaking into his thoughts.

"Then we'd best be off," he replied, giving her a smile as he held out her cloak.

Jonathan took the lead as they entered the house, obviously anxious to seek out Margaret and assure himself that she had survived an afternoon of his mother's incessant questions and prying. He looked back at Teddi in surprise when he didn't see either his mother or Margaret in the parlor or dining room. Teddi followed behind him, but they both stopped in their tracks when they heard the sound of laughter coming from the kitchen. It was Isabelle and Margaret, and they certainly seemed to be enjoying themselves.

"What are you two doing in the kitchen?" Jonathan inquired while shooting Margaret an inquisitive glance.

"I saw that look, Jonathan. Your bride-to-be is just fine. In fact, she's more than fine; she's wonderful. We were just discussing how many children you two were hoping to have," Isabelle proclaimed.

Jonathan moved back from the kitchen door, obviously stunned by the turn of events. "Do I get any say-so in this matter, or is it solely up to you and my mother?" Jonathan inquired, the look of surprise still etched on his face.

All of them were enjoying a laugh at Jonathan's expense when Clayton entered the house. "What's going on in here? You folks having a party, and I wasn't invited?" he asked.

"I wouldn't call it a party. It seems that Mother and Margaret have spent the afternoon making decisions regarding how many children we should have. For some reason I thought Margaret might want to consult with *me* about the subject of children rather than Mother," Jonathan explained facetiously.

"We discussed much more than that. Why don't we all go into the parlor," Isabelle suggested, pulling off her apron and bidding Margaret do the same. Once the group was seated, Isabelle shifted in her seat so that she could face all of them. "I don't plan to go into all the details of our discussion, but I do want my family to know that I'm ashamed of my behavior. I asked Margaret's forgiveness, and although I'm not sure I would have been so kindhearted, she has accepted my apology.

"Teddi, I'm sorry that I didn't take your advice and teaching to heart when you first talked to me about forgiveness. It would have saved Margaret from once again being mistreated by an insensitive Christian—namely, me! I hope I've learned my lesson. And although Jonathan has already been very clear that he planned to marry Margaret no matter what my objection, I want you both to know that I will be exceedingly proud to have Margaret as a member of our family. Now that I've admitted my shortcomings to Margaret and asked her forgiveness, I feel I must also ask you to do the same, Jona—"

"No, no, that's not necessary, Mother," Jonathan interrupted, obviously quite moved by his mother's sincere comments.

"Then at least let me say that I am very proud of you. Your father and I always prayed that our children would grow into adults who actually lived what Christ taught. You children do it much better than I ever have, and I am exceedingly blessed to have all of you.

"I'm finished with all this serious talk. Margaret and I have been hard at work in the kitchen, and I think it's time we all partake," Isabelle said, rising from her chair with a flourish.

"Let's hope that things go this smoothly for us tomorrow night," Phillip murmured to Teddi as they walked into the dining room.

sixteen

All day Wednesday, Phillip attempted to keep himself composed, wondering how he could possibly preach a sermon in a few hours. Teddi had struggled to help him focus on the message he would deliver, but maintaining his concentration had been difficult. Finally, she had joined him in his office at the hospital, making several suggestions as she pointed out Scripture verses to reinforce her ideas.

The singing during the church service was particularly inspiring, and Phillip was pleased to see that there were more people at the Wednesday night meeting than generally attended. It was probably due to the holiday season—folks always seemed to remember the importance of church attendance at Christmas and Easter, he realized.

Stepping up to the podium, Phillip placed his Bible in front of him, cleared his throat, and stared out into the sea of faces; all eyes were focused on him.

"I want to talk to you about leading more Christlike lives. For those of you who call yourselves Christians, I thought tonight might be an excellent opportunity to take personal inventory of how your life compares to that of Jesus Christ. For example, do you compromise Christ's teachings in your day-to-day life? Do you think that if nobody sees you cheat or steal, it doesn't matter? Do you think that when you mistreat another member of the human race, you're following Christ's example? Do you think your idle gossip doesn't constitute sin? Do you think your unforgiving attitudes go unnoticed? Do you think that when you covet another man's possessions, it's all right because you deserve more than you have?"

Phillip continued with the list of questions, watching as members of the congregation squirmed and looked away, unable to meet his eyes when the arrow of truth pierced their hearts. When he had finished the questions, he placed his written list in front of him on a metal plate. Taking a burning candle from its holder, he touched the flame to the pages and watched until the fire had consumed them, leaving nothing but ashes on the plate.

"For those of you who are Christians, your sins are like those sheets of paper. Once you've asked God's forgiveness and have truly repented, your sin is gone, forgotten, wiped away. That's a difficult concept for us to understand because we humans have a great deal of difficulty forgiving others and forgetting what they've done to us; but aren't we thankful for a God who will do that for us? Now, for anyone here who hasn't accepted Christ, this gift can be yours—it's a free gift from your Creator. All you must do is accept it. But listen carefully: If you don't take that step and actually accept God's gift of salvation, your sins remain *your personal baggage*. They aren't erased or turned into ash like those sheets of paper on the plate; no, they are yours to carry with you to the grave and beyond."

He had the attention of the congregation, although he wasn't sure they were happy with his message. Most of them had probably come to church expecting to hear a sermon relating to the birth of Christ, something more in keeping with the season. But Teddi had been right; he needed to preach what was in his heart, and that's what he had done.

At the end of the sermon Phillip was astounded by the number of his parishioners who came forward and prayed for forgiveness, wanting to clear the slate and make a fresh attempt at leading a Christian life. Even more wonderful was the fact that three people made their way to him and asked how they could have Christ as their personal Savior, sure there must be more they must do in order to receive such an extraordinary gift.

"This has been quite a night," Phillip said to Teddi shortly after the service. "No matter what Herbert has to say, I know that God has been at work in this matter."

"Isn't it wonderful? I'm thrilled at what happened here tonight. Please don't let your meeting with Herbert spoil the amazing things that just occurred."

"I won't," he promised. "I'll talk to you in the morning," he added before walking off toward his office.

"I think I'll join you for that meeting with Herbert," Clayton said as Phillip neared the small antechamber at the back of the church. The general placed his arm across Phillip's shoulder as the two of them entered the room.

"Well, aren't you two a sight," Herbert sneered from the doorway. "Have you come to your senses, Hamilton?"

"I have indeed," Phillip replied. "I'll not be coerced by your bullying tactics, and if you're hoping to stick to your plan and marry Teddi, you'd better move quickly. Otherwise, she and I may be married before you have time to file your charges. That's my answer. I have nothing further to say."

"You're going to be sorry. You'll be thrown out of the army, and I'll make it my mission to destroy you," Herbert snarled as he pushed by both men and left the church with the sound of the slamming door reverberating through the sanctuary.

&

It was shortly before noon the next day when Clayton entered the hospital and advised Phillip that Helen and Herbert had submitted sworn statements. After reviewing the documents, Colonel Cartwright determined that charges should be filed against Phillip. However, General Yorke had already received assurance that the process would move forward as quickly as possible.

"Colonel Cartwright is in charge of the proceedings. He has given his word that the board will convene on Friday. I told him I would be surprised if it took more than a few hours. Captain Pauley will act as your counsel; he'll come here to meet with you at two o'clock this afternoon. Jonathan, George, and I plan to arrive at two-thirty to meet with both of you and go over our testimony."

"You've been busy this morning. I can't believe all you've accomplished in such a short time. Do you think there's a possibility that Herbert will object to the trial taking place so rapidly?" Phillip asked. "I do want to get this over with."

"The paperwork he signed contains a waiver declaring that he will agree to the time and date of the hearing. It also contains a clause stating that at the time the complaint was signed, the complainant who brought the charges possessed sufficient evidence to immediately go to hearing. If he objects, his complaint will be dismissed. Fortunately, this decreases the amount of time he'll have to spread the word about town, which is all the better for us. I'd like to avoid having this thing turn into a spectacle. When you meet with Captain Pauley, you might want to suggest that he talk with Mattie—about her testimony," the general suggested.

"No. I think I'll just leave that in God's hands," Phillip replied.

&

The room was hushed, Herbert and Helen sitting side by side at a wooden table only a few feet from where Phillip now sat beside Captain Pauley. General Yorke's desire that the hearing be a quiet affair had fallen flat. Every chair was occupied, while additional spectators stood crowded at the rear of the room; they all appeared anxious to hear the offensive details. The board members were seated at a long, narrow table facing the crowded room, each of them appearing uncomfortable with the size of the crowd assembled before them.

Colonel Cartwright cleared his throat, struck his wooden gavel on the table, and advised all in attendance that the matter would proceed henceforth. Looking toward Herbert, he instructed him to commence with his case against Captain Hamilton.

At Herbert's instruction, Helen moved to the witness chair and, after being sworn to tell the truth, began answering Herbert's questions. A murmuring of voices erupted as Helen staunchly proclaimed that her life had been left in ruins the night of the masquerade ball. Obviously anxious to hear all of the details, the crowd hushed when she once again began to speak. A tear slid down her cheek as she declared that Captain Hamilton had forced her into his sleigh. Herbert gallantly rushed to offer his handkerchief as she continued with her story, stating that Phillip had taken advantage of her inability to fight him off. A small sob erupted as Helen wiped her eyes and then asserted to the board that Phillip had spoken harsh words to her.

"Captain Hamilton said that he would *never* give up his plan to marry Teddi Yorke. He told me that marrying into the Yorke family would help his military career while I had nothing of value to bring to a marriage. He did say, however, that he would enjoy having me as his mistress once he married Teddi," Helen averred.

Once again, gasps of surprise and murmuring voices filled the courtroom. Colonel Cartwright's gavel rapped on the oak table as he called for silence in the room.

"You may continue, Miss Hanson," Herbert sympathetically encouraged.

Helen nodded her head, wiped her nose, and looked out at the crowd. *"Now* Captain Hamilton denies all of the horrid things he did to me. But I have a witness who will tell you that I speak the truth," Helen purred, having now turned her full attention to the members of the board. "That's all I have to tell you, gentlemen. I know you'll do the right thing." She batted her eyelashes, gave them a seductive smile, and stepped down from the witness chair.

"Let's hear from your corroborating witness, Mr. Albright," Colonel Cartwright directed.

Herbert turned toward the roomful of spectators. "Mattie Fielding, step forward."

All eyes scanned the room waiting, anticipating, eager to hear what little Mattie Fielding would tell them. The rustling of feet and scraping of chairs were finally rewarded as Mattie moved from among the onlookers at the rear of the room and walked toward the witness chair. Once seated, she quickly scanned the spectators and then allowed her gaze to rest upon Phillip for a brief moment.

Herbert vaulted out of his chair, obviously anxious to complete his unconscionable prosecution so he could bask in the glory of his unjustified victory. After casting a depraved look in Phillip's direction, he turned his attention toward Mattie, who sat facing him, her fingers gripping the arms of the wooden chair with such intensity that her knuckles had turned white.

"Good morning, Mattie," he greeted in a soft and amiable voice.

She nodded but remained silent as he padded about the room in front of her—a cat cornering his prey, relishing the moment before moving in for the kill. She squirmed in her seat and then hunched down as if succumbing to a predator.

"Now then, Mattie, since you appear somewhat disconcerted, why don't I help you along? I'll ask you questions that you can simply answer yes or no to make this easier for you. Would you like that?"

Mattie nodded her bowed head in agreement.

"Did you attend the masquerade ball at the theater last Saturday night?"

"Yes," came her whispered reply.

"Just so the board is certain you can identify Captain Phillip Hamilton, would you please point to him?"

Mattie raised her head and quickly pointed toward Phillip.

"Thank you, Mattie. You attended the ball in the company of Helen Hanson. Is that correct?"

Mattie shook her head affirmatively. "Helen and you," she added.

"Yes, and we quickly separated company, didn't we? You and Helen went off in search of Captain Hamilton because he told Helen that he would meet her at the party, isn't that correct?"

"We went to search for Captain Hamilton, but—"

"Objection. She can't testify as to what Captain Hamilton and Miss Hanson may have discussed. Both parties are present in court. If Mr. Albright wants that information before the board, let him ask one of them," Captain Pauley interjected.

"Oh, never mind. You do agree that you and Helen parted company with me," he angrily continued before Colonel Cartwright could rule on the objection.

"Did you see Helen Hanson and Phillip Hamilton leave the party and go outside that night?"

"Yes."

"And did you see them get into Captain Hamilton's sleigh?"

"Yes," she quietly replied.

"And where were you when you observed this?"

"His sleigh was sitting beside the shed in back of the theater. I was inside the shed," she meekly replied.

"But the door was open, and you could hear everything that was said?"

"Oh, yes," she replied, her voice now growing stronger. "Every single word."

"That is all. You may step down," Herbert said.

"Not so fast, Mr. Albright. I want to cross-examine this

witness," Captain Pauley stated while rising from his chair.

"Go right ahead. You'll only be helping to dig your client's grave," he whispered as Captain Pauley walked forward.

Captain Pauley ignored Herbert's remark and approached the witness stand, giving Mattie an encouraging smile. "You know that you are under oath and sworn to tell the truth, Miss Fielding?" he asked as he stood at one side of her chair.

"Yes, sir, and I've spoken nothing but the truth," Mattie avowed.

Herbert nodded his head, a smile spreading across his face. He turned toward the crowd, obviously hoping that Mattie's declaration had impressed them.

"Good. Now, you said you could hear everything that was said between Captain Hamilton and Miss Hanson while they were in the sleigh, and from where you were positioned, I don't doubt that. But could you tell me, Mattie, *why* you followed Helen and Captain Hamilton outdoors on that cold night?"

Mattie shifted in the chair. "Because Helen told me to," she replied.

"I see. And did she tell you why she wanted you to hide outside and listen?"

"So I could be a witness to the fact that she and Captain Hamilton actually were outside in the sleigh for a long time."

Captain Pauley nodded his head. "And now I'd like you to tell this board exactly what you heard that night."

Mattie gazed toward Helen and then toward Phillip. She took a deep breath, and in a calm, steady voice, she told the board of Helen's plan of blackmail, slander, and seduction, as well as her subsequent lack of success. Step by step, she disclosed the plot contrived by Herbert and Helen and how she, as Helen's friend, had been pressured into assisting with the plan.

"Herbert wants to marry Teddi Yorke, and Helen wants to

marry Captain Hamilton. They thought this plan would succeed in getting both of them what they wanted," Mattie stated, keeping her gaze upon Captain Pauley.

"She's a liar!" Herbert retorted.

"I'm not lying, sir. And had it not been for the fact that on Wednesday night I accepted the Lord Jesus Christ as my Savior, I *would* be sitting here telling you exactly what Herbert and Helen told me to say. But I can't do that now, Helen," she said, turning toward her old friend. "It's wrong, don't you see?"

A scarlet-faced Helen jumped from her chair and ran out of the room as Herbert stared after her in disbelief.

"I'll dismiss the charges," Herbert announced as he jumped out of his chair.

"In that case I'll release this board from further duty. . . . Not so fast, Captain Albright," Colonel Cartwright called out as Herbert began to turn and leave the courtroom. "Until such time as a board can be convened to investigate your conduct in this matter, you are immediately confined to officers' quarters on this military post. Your commanding officer at Fort Brown will be notified of these proceedings and the probability that you will not be returning to his command. On a personal note, Captain Albright, I might suggest that you and Miss Hanson would make a lovely couple. In all likelihood, you'll soon be relieved of your military obligations, and I, for one, certainly think you deserve each other," Colonel Cartwright remarked dryly as members of the community slowly filed out of the room, nodding their heads in agreement.

seventeen

General Yorke smiled as he walked to the parlor windows and pulled back the curtain. "Looks like we're going to get us a good snow. It's flurrying already, and those are some mighty big snow clouds looming overhead."

"Clayton! You've been saying that for days now. Every time we get a few flurries, you predict a major snowstorm. It's wishful thinking on your part. You can come help me with these boxes. Staring out the window isn't going to make it snow," Isabelle said with authority.

"I thought Jonathan was going to help you sort through these decorations weeks ago," Clayton replied as he carried the boxes into the parlor.

"He seemed to lose interest once he met Margaret," his wife said with a smile. "I still wish they would wait so that there would be time to plan for a formal wedding. A Christmas wedding would be such fun compared to the small ceremony they've planned," Isabelle stated.

"Now, Isabelle, I think you can find more than enough to keep you busy during the holiday season without planning a wedding," Clayton replied. "Of course, you may be able to convince Teddi to have a Christmas wedding."

"What's this about convincing me of something?" Teddi asked as she and Phillip walked into the house.

"Your mother is lamenting the fact that there wasn't enough time to plan a large wedding for Jonathan and Margaret. She thinks making arrangements for a big Christmas wedding would give her great enjoyment, so I told her she might take it up with you. Perhaps the two of you would like to plan on a large Christmas wedding next year?" Clayton asked.

"Father! You weren't supposed to tell. We wanted our wedding announcement to be a surprise," Teddi scolded.

"Phillip has asked you to marry him?" Isabelle asked with a look of amazement on her face. "Why didn't you tell me? How long have you known, Clayton?"

"You see, Teddi? I didn't betray your confidence. Seems I remember something like this happening not so long ago. Remember when your mother thought I had betrayed your confidence by telling Phillip about your broken engagement? You both seem to think I can't keep a secret, when really it's the two of you who jump to conclusions and tell everything you know," he replied as his boisterous laughter filled the room.

Phillip put his arm around Teddi's shoulder. "We can still make the announcement after we've finished decorating the tree this evening. George, Jonathan, and Margaret don't yet know of our plans. It will still be a celebration," he promised.

"Well, I suppose you know that I couldn't be more delighted that you're going to become a member of our family, Phillip. Just think—your wedding will be a grand opportunity for us to see your parents again. They *will* be coming for the wedding, won't they? Have you already agreed on a date? A Christmas wedding is always so beautiful, Teddi, but if you think you'd prefer to marry in the spring or summer, I can certainly have everything ready in time," Isabelle rattled on.

"We haven't actually settled on a date, Isabelle, but if you're going to hold out for a Christmas wedding, it will have to be this year. I'm not about to wait a year before making your daughter my wife," Phillip staunchly replied as he squeezed Teddi's hand.

"You could have a double wedding with Margaret and Jonathan. . . ."

"No, mother, we are *not* getting married next week. That's much too soon. I understand why Jonathan and Margaret are hurrying their plans. They have good reason, but I think Phillip and I would prefer to take a little time to enjoy preparing for our wedding."

"Hrmmph! Let me interpret that for you, Phillip," Clayton offered. "Taking time to enjoy preparing for the wedding means your fiancée wants time enough to plan the *perfect* wedding, one that she believes will provide her with enough memories to last a lifetime. You, my boy, will have very little to say about the matter, and *I* will have even less. In fact, my input will consist of providing adequate funds to cover the costs of what will likely turn into an extravaganza."

"You're exaggerating, Clayton," Isabelle chastised. "It may turn into a gala event, but I doubt Teddi would go so far as to create an extravaganza."

"Just wait!" Clayton warned as Jonathan and Margaret walked in the front door, covered with snow.

"It's no longer flurries falling out there," Jonathan announced, stomping his feet while brushing snowflakes from Margaret's coat.

"Where's George?" Clayton asked. "I haven't seen him since the noon meal."

"He said he was going down to the river with some of the soldiers. They were going to cut ice for the icehouse," Teddi replied. "I told him to check with you, that I didn't think the ice would be thick enough yet."

"He knows better. That river won't be frozen thick enough to cut ice blocks until the end of January. My guess is he's down there ice-skating," Clayton replied.

It was only minutes later when George returned, his ice skates tied together and thrown over his shoulder. "Look who I brought along," he announced, pulling Mattie forward. "The ice wasn't thick enough to cut, so I went into town for a couple of Christmas presents. There was Mattie at one of the stores, and I asked her to join us," George announced.

"We're delighted to have you, Mattie. Your parents don't mind if you spend Christmas Eve with us?" Isabelle kindly inquired.

"No. Since my pa died, my mother isn't interested in much of anything, especially celebrating holidays. She doesn't care that I'm here," Mattie answered docilely.

"Well, we're pleased to have you here to help us celebrate Christ's birth, Mattie," Clayton said with a welcoming smile. "You just dig in there and help with those ornaments. I'm sure that George will be glad to let you do his share of the work."

"Yep, sure will. Is supper about ready?" George asked, rubbing his stomach as though he were starving.

"Dinner will be ready by the time you've finished sorting through the ornaments. It's got to be done before we decorate the tree. By the time you finish, we'll be ready to eat," Isabelle replied, shooing him toward the boxes while the rest of them laughed at her antics. "There may be some of Jonathan's old homemade ornaments you'd like to take for your tree next Christmas, Margaret," Isabelle offered as she hurried off toward the kitchen.

"I doubt that," Jonathan replied, pulling out a box that had been carefully labeled with his name. There were ornaments made of pinecones, milk pods, and other sundry reflections of nature, most of them now falling apart. Teddi held up one of her prized creations, which had been reduced to shriveled berries inside half a walnut shell. They laughed and reminisced while digging through the boxes, each of them quick to tell the others the history of a particular ornament before it was carefully tucked back into the box.

"I think we're ready for dinner," Isabelle announced. "You should be finished by now, I would think. Give me the trash, and I'll ask Florence to toss it in the fireplace."

Each of them looked at the other and began to laugh.

"There is no trash, Mother. After spending the last hour telling the wonderful stories that go with these ornaments, we couldn't throw any of them away."

"You see, Clayton, it isn't such an easy thing to do. Your father's after me all the time to get rid of things. He says that if you're in the military, you need to travel light, but I say that a family needs its memories!"

"And after listening to our children this afternoon, I'd have to agree. I think it would make for a special tree if you used those old ornaments one last time this year," Clayton suggested.

Teddi laughed at the suggestion. "I don't think Mother would want her majestic tree covered with these dilapidated decorations."

"You're wrong about that, dear. I think it would make for a beautiful tree," Isabelle replied.

Once they had finished dinner, the group of young people decorated the tree while Isabelle and Clayton directed the proceedings. There was just enough time to light the candles for one glimpse of the tree before leaving for church services.

Sleighs were gathering around the chapel by the time they arrived, and Christmas greetings were being exchanged as people entered the church and were seated. The pews were almost full when the worshipers began to sing Christmas carols and to celebrate Christ's birth. Then, as midnight edged closer, each person walked down the aisle carrying a small, lighted candle, received communion, and left the church, with the trail of flickering light providing a festive illumination for the congregation as they bid each other Merry Christmas before heading home.

❧

"It was a beautiful way to celebrate Christmas Eve," Teddi said as she and Phillip arrived back at the Yorkes' quarters. "Mother said I was to invite you in for coffee and cookies."

"It's not too late?"

"Not on Christmas Eve. Everyone else is already inside!"

The snow had ceased falling, and a full moon surrounded by a myriad of stars shone down on the fresh blanket of glistening snow. Phillip tugged on the reins, and the horses snorted and shook their heads as they came to a halt.

As they reached the porch and Phillip opened the door, a grin spread across his face. "I have a special gift I want to give you—a surprise. Could we go into the parlor by ourselves for just a few moments?" he asked while reaching into his pocket and retrieving a small box wrapped in brown paper and adorned with a sprig of holly.

"My ring?" she asked, leading the way into the parlor.

The rest of the family was gathered around the dining-room table, seemingly unaware of the newly arrived couple now standing by the Christmas tree.

"No. That wouldn't be a surprise—you already know about your ring," he replied.

Teddi carefully removed the sprig of holly, untied the thin red ribbon, and lifted off the lid. Tucked into a small piece of red satin was a tiny ice-skate charm. "Oh, Phillip!" was all that she could manage as she lifted the charm from its snug resting place.

"It's wonderful! How did you ever—?" She could say nothing else, a lump rising in her throat.

"Margaret's father found a jeweler in Kansas City who said he could craft the charm and have it delivered by Christmas. I briefly considered a sleigh bell, but Jonathan has given me his word that yours will be returned. I decided upon an ice-skate because the day of the ice-skating party is the day I knew that I truly loved you."

"It is? I didn't know that."

"That's the day I knew that you were a woman of virtue, the woman with whom I wanted to share my life," he said, his eyes filled with adoration.

"Thank you, Phillip. You couldn't have given me a more perfect gift. And I have something for you. Wait here," she said, leaving the room and returning a few moments later. She carried a large, wooden box without a lid. Inside the box was a lumpy, folded sleigh blanket, tied with a thin cord.

He gave the odd-looking package a questioning look, and then glanced back at Teddi.

"Go ahead—open it," she instructed merrily.

Phillip tentatively unknotted the twine and pulled back the gray, wool blanket. "Sleigh bells!" he shouted joyfully. Each of the two leather straps sported at least thirty bells, all jingling noisily as Phillip pulled them out of the blanket. "You got me sleigh bells! Come on—let's go outside and put them on the horses," he said, pulling her to her feet.

"We'll be right back," Teddi called over her shoulder toward the dining room as the two of them rushed out the door, oblivious to the cold night air.

"They're wonderful, just like you," Phillip delightedly stated as he finished attaching the jingling leather straps to the team of horses.

Pulling her close, he stood back and gave the sleigh one final look of appraisal before nodding his head in satisfaction. Wrapping his arms around her, he leaned forward and gently kissed her lips. "Merry Christmas, my love. The sleigh bells are grand, but *you* are truly God's splendid gift to me," he whispered.

A Letter To Our Readers

Dear Reader:

In order that we might better contribute to your reading enjoyment, we would appreciate your taking a few minutes to respond to the following questions. We welcome your comments and read each form and letter we receive. When completed, please return to the following:

Rebecca Germany, Fiction Editor
Heartsong Presents
PO Box 719
Uhrichsville, Ohio 44683

1. Did you enjoy reading *Sleigh Bells?*
    ❑ Very much. I would like to see more books
       by this author!
    ❑ Moderately
       I would have enjoyed it more if _____

    _____

    _____

2. Are you a member of **Heartsong Presents**? Yes ❑ No ❑
    If no, where did you purchase this book? _____

    _____

3. How would you rate, on a scale from 1 (poor) to 5 (superior),
    the cover design? _____

4. On a scale from 1 (poor) to 10 (superior), please rate the
    following elements.

    _____ Heroine   _____ Plot

    _____ Hero   _____ Inspirational theme

    _____ Setting   _____ Secondary characters

5. These characters were special because_____

_____

_____

6. How has this book inspired your life?_____

_____

_____

7. What settings would you like to see covered in future **Heartsong Presents** books?_____

_____

_____

8. What are some inspirational themes you would like to see treated in future books?_____

_____

_____

9. Would you be interested in reading other **Heartsong Presents** titles?   Yes ❏   No ❏

10. Please check your age range:
    ❏ Under 18   ❏ 18-24   ❏ 25-34
    ❏ 35-45   ❏ 46-55   ❏ Over 55

11. How many hours per week do you read?_____

Name _____

Occupation _____

Address _____

City _____ State _____ Zip _____

Greece. . .a land of historic enchantment and romance. . . a perfect place for love. From the pen of Melanie Panagiotopoulos, a resident of Athens, come four thrilling love stories. . .

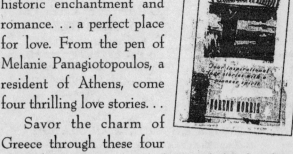

Savor the charm of Greece through these four unique stories. Experience the search for the ultimate gift of love—between a man and a woman and from the God whose gifts are good and perfect.

paperback, 464 pages, 5 ³⁄₁₆" x 8"

❤ ❤ ❤ ❤ ❤ ❤ ❤ ❤ ❤ ❤ ❤ ❤ ❤ ❤ ❤ ❤

❤ ❤ ❤ ❤ ❤ ❤ ❤ ❤ ❤ ❤ ❤ ❤ ❤ ❤ ❤ ❤

·······Presents·······

Hearts♥ng Presents
Love Stories Are Rated G!

That's for godly, gratifying, and of course, great! If you love a thrilling love story, but don't appreciate the sordidness of some popular paperback romances, **Heartsong Presents** is for you. In fact, **Heartsong Presents** is the *only inspirational romance book club* featuring love stories where Christian faith is the primary ingredient in a marriage relationship.

Sign up today to receive your first set of four, never before published Christian romances. Send no money now; you will receive a bill with the first shipment. You may cancel at any time without obligation, and if you aren't completely satisfied with any selection, you may return the books for an immediate refund!

Imagine. . .four new romances every four weeks—two historical, two contemporary—with men and women like you who long to meet the one God has chosen as the love of their lives. . . all for the low price of $9.97 postpaid.

To join, simply complete the coupon below and mail to the address provided. **Heartsong Presents** romances are rated G for another reason: They'll arrive *Godspeed!*